Bond Book

D0875769

COOPER'S REVENGE

COOPER'S REVENGE

•

Joe Burkett

AVALON BOOKS
NEW YORK

PRINTED IN THE UNITED STATES OF AMERICA
ON ACID-FREE PAPER
BY HADDON CRAFTSMEN, BLOOMSBURG, PENNSYLVANIA

To my grandfather, Jessie Lee Burkett,
who told me many stories,
one of which inspired me to write this book.

Chapter One

Bright sunlight illuminated the kitchen-and-parlor side of the log, dogtrot house as Bell Cooper went about preparing a large dinner. Summer heat, combined with that of the wood stove, dampened her tan face and neck with perspiration, and a lock of dark hair stuck attractively to her forehead. She always fixed for several at noon on Tuesdays and Fridays because she didn't know how many, if any, would be aboard the stage which stopped for a change of horses twice weekly at the homestead on its runs between Maple Springs, Texas and Bentosa, Louisiana. Through the window by the sideboard and range Bell watched her and Tom's boy on the errand to the woodshed she'd sent him on.

The spitting image of his strong, sandy-haired fa-

1

ther, five-year-old Stanly was big for his age, and as he carried a considerable amount of stove wood he heard the chirping of a wren somewhere in the vicinity of the barn, crib, and corrals. Maybe later, when his dad and the hired hand, Jonas, returned from town, he might get the two men to agree for him to join them in going out to mark the new broods of pigs. He always liked to watch them and Josie, the brindle cur dog which was now at his heels, work the stock ranging in the lush East Texas forest.

Once on a trip the boy hadn't been on, Jonas roped a big sow that was charging Tom, and another time— Stan had seen this himself—Josie saved Jonas from their big Hereford bull by busting him good and proper.

Bell thanked her son upon depositing the load of fuel in the wood box near the stove. After making certain she had no more chores for him, Stanly went back out into the coolness of the open hallway which divided the two main sections of the cabin. He tugged playfully at Josie's muzzle and she wagged her tail and smiled at him. Then the boy looked up at the noise of a foursome trotting up the lane to their place from the main wagon road; they came slanting across the yard, scattering some of his mama's chickens that were hunting insects or other such forage.

He stepped back in and announced, "Ma, there's riders comin'."

"Who?" Bell asked, thinking the last thing she needed was company on such a busy day.

"Don't know 'em. One's got a humongous hat, though."

Sighing, she followed Stan outside, wiping face and hands on her flour-sack apron. She wished Tom and Jonas hadn't gone to town on a stage day, but she and Stan had handled the job before, and a lot of supplies were needed while there was produce to trade.

At the edge of the porch Bell Cooper determined quickly that she didn't like these four men. Thus she was nervous. Trying not to show her insecurity, she greeted them as they drew up abreast.

The one who spoke was sinewy and not beyond middle age, yet his hair beneath a broad-brimmed hat was strangely white. "Ma'am, this the Circle C?"

Bell nodded, and the questioner put forth, "The stage be by here around twelve, will it?"

Good manners made Stan remain quiet while his ma affirmed the man's second query. Something about Bell's tone and the way her arm draped protectively around his shoulders told the boy she was uncomfortable, and his own little heart sped up as he looked at the mean eyes of the squatty fellow in the big straw sombrero. He was a Mexican in dirty clothing with a droopy mustache on a pocked, gray face.

Likewise the flaxen-haired man who spoke for the group could sense Bell's nervousness, and he inquired in a friendly way if her husband, Cooper, was at home—he and his gang had invested too much time and effort in feeling this job out to screw it up now.

"No, but he should be back any minute." It was a lie, for Tom and Jonas, she knew, could not hope to be back before noon on the wagon trip. Although they had left at dawn, it would take pretty near half a day. Probably longer.

Bell unconsciously took a step back as the man dismounted without being told to alight. His voice became hard, befitting the belligerent outlaw leader he was. "I'm Zed Rodel. You just mind what we say, little lady."

Her first impulse was to grab up Stanly and retreat to the living room where her deceased father's old flintlock hung—even the boy had heard of Zed Rodel, a murdering thief who, with his bunch, had raised Cain from the Mississippi River all the way to San Antonio, and the Indian Territory to the Rio Grande! Yet the youngest of the four men suddenly had a Colt in his hand.

"Fast," Rodel addressed him by his nickname, "cover her till we make sure the place is clear. Blue, you check the other cabin and outbuildings."

In a flash Rodel and the Mexican, Miguel Fuantez, were going through the house with drawn revolvers. Choctaw Blue, a half-breed from the Nations who got his handle from the bluish-black smudge in the flesh of his left cheek, caused by a lawman's gun going off near his face, reined his mount off to follow orders. A Sharps carbine was in his hand. Stan caught a glimpse of the hideous blemish when the Indian's long hair flew back from his angular face, and the child's blood ran cold. Nevertheless, under the steady pistol of the young man covering him and his mother, the boy didn't whimper or squirm. He wouldn't let them know he was afraid.

Bell was also scared, but her features remained stoic. She knew only Rodel by name; the bandit had been talked of by some in her presence. His depredations were well known. *Lord, if Tom and Jonas had known these men were in the area they would have never left us alone!* Yet, now . . .

"What do ya want?" she demanded when Rodel and the Mexican found the house void of other occupants and herded her and the boy roughly into the kitchen. Josie watched from the open door, knowing all was not well, yet not certain of what action to take.

None of the trio with the captives replied. Each knew what they were after—the express box with six thousand dollars in it that would be on the coach bound for the Maple Springs First National Bank. They brought their long guns inside the house to be ready for anything.

Zed was his confident self, meaning to be certain of every minute detail. Fast Luke Bledsoe relaxed in a straight chair and exposed his dusty-red hair while wiping the sweat from his hatband. Miguel was robust, striding about the long room with prying eyes, all the while eating a piece of corn bread and helping himself to the fried potatoes that Bell had moved to the side of the stove.

"You got wheeskey here, woman?" Miguel demanded with a full mouth.

Bell was anything save a weak female, emotionally *or* physically, and had given thought to using the sizzling skillet of potatoes and lard as a weapon, yet hadn't because there was Stanly to think of. "There's some for medicinal purposes in the crib," she said evenly.

"Ain't gonna be no liquor consumed till this job's over and done." Zed Rodel banished the happy look from Miguel's eyes. Zed's old man had been an abusive drunk from whom he'd run away at sixteen, so miraculously Rodel didn't take to alcohol—loathed it, in fact. Otherwise, Zed was a hard man who lived by a loose moral code, if one at all.

The only one of his group he had a bit of fear of was Fast Bledsoe, for the young man's lean stature and long arms made him adept in the drawing of a six-gun and getting it into play—accurately. Rodel could sense Bledsoe's occasional desire to ramrod the gang himself, and the outlaw leader wondered if he would one day have to back-shoot the little sneak.

Until it came to that, Zed treated him as second in command, for he was a valuable asset. When or if such was ever called for, he would handle it like a catamount—a surprise attack—not straight up front like a grizzly. Zed knew his limitations with a hogleg, and he figured it was better to be sneaky and alive than prideful and dead.

Miguel Fuantez just grunted submissively at the rebuke about the liquor, and Choctaw Blue entered the house to speak: "No one around. The other cabin must be for the hired man."

"Fine. Put up our horses so they won't be seen. Then c'mon back," Rodel directed, and the man was immediately gone.

Stan had inherited a proud braveness from his father. "You fellas won't get away with this!"

"Hush, Stan," Bell said.

Fast Bledsoe leaned menacingly toward the kid. "Listen to your ma, boy. Seen and not heard, ya know."

"I ain't afraid of you," Stan retorted, though secretly he wanted his pa there, hoped he'd return early for some odd reason.

Slipping his pistol suddenly from its holster low on his hip, Bledsoe enjoyed seeing the boy and his mother's eyes grow large as he trained it on Stan's face. Slowly, after the long space of several heartbeats, he eased the hammer back down and surmised before putting the Colt away, "You be good, and I'll let ya watch me in action after a while with this iron. I got my name from gun handlin', ya know."

Miguel's mind went from whiskey to something else. He swallowed the last of his food and moved closer to Bell, commenting, "*Amigos,* this ees a very fine *señora*, no?"

Bledsoe and Rodel laughed in an ugly way and Bell jerked her face back from that of the smelly outlaw. She could see Stan was scared badly now, and she inched backward. "Let my son go outside. Please, he's only a boy." She desperately wanted him away from this. She knew what was about to take place: she had feared it from the beginning.

Zed and Bledsoe were standing expectantly now. The first looked at his gold watch, an expensive time-piece taken off a wealthy riverman in Nacogdoches. He grinned an evil grin from weathered lips. "The boy stays where we can keep an eye on 'im." To his men who were present, he stated, "Got little over an hour 'fore time for the coach. I reckon there's time for some entertainment."

The nervous cur was growling low at the open door-way to the dogtrot as Miguel began pawing at the lovely Bell Cooper, pressed against the log wall beside the hot range. The woman's stomach rolled over at the brute's touch and she struggled to keep his dirty mouth away from hers, all the time thinking frantically of her loving husband, their life together, the children.

The other two men had turned to do away with the threatening animal when their attention was averted by something else.

"Get away from my mama!" shrilled Stan, rushing forward to light into Miguel with his fists.

A Spanish oath, then the boy was flung back from the impact of Miguel's knuckles on his small round face. There came a sharp crack as Stan's head hit the edge of the plank table, and Bell erupted with a mother's fury. Fast Bledsoe reached for his pistol a fraction of a second before Rodel upon seeing the woman's intention, and had nearly cleared leather before the snarling Josie lunged into him. Miguel pivoted back to Bell to be met by a long cooking fork aimed at his fat belly.

The Mexican lost his sombrero as he staggered back, clutching at his ruined guts and whining like a kicked pup. Bledsoe's gun arm was occupied by the sharp fangs of the cur, and as boots pounded on the porch then along the dogtrot, Zed sent a .45 slug into Bell's heart. She fell against the wall with a sigh, to slide to the floor and into the next world.

Now Choctaw Blue was the kind of strong, stocky gent who'd bring a knife to a gunfight any day—he was that good with one—and he'd heard the calamity on the way back from the barn. He had come on the run, black hair trailing wildly back from under his flat-brimmed hat with its round, creaseless crown. The Arkansas toothpick from his belt was point up in his hand.

It was that large blade Rodel saw used to disengage the cur from Bledsoe's arm. The Indian stood spread-legged in the doorway then, watching his thrown weapon bleed the life out of the dog's pierced chest. Carefully he walked forward with his right hand on the butt of the Smith & Wesson at his hip.

No one answered his question of "What just happened here?" until both the woman and child were checked for life and found dead. Then it was the excited Bledsoe who explained everything while Zed saw to the young man's hurt forearm. Blue heard him out as he tried to staunch the flow of blood from Miguel's tormented guts.

"We're in a heap of trouble now!" he exclaimed, stepping back from the Mexican when he was done. "I oughtta finish ya myself. You got us into this!"

Miguel hushed his alternate cursing and praying and shrank further into the cowhide couch he lay on. "Zed, Fast, keep this *loco* away from me!"

Rodel was mad. "What's the matter with you, Blue?"

The Indian shook his head, regretting joining this trio on their last trip north. "Hurt a settler woman, and the law and ever'body else will hunt you like a rogue bear! This Cooper may be like the pox to us when he sees this!" He pointed to the woman and child.

Bledsoe gave that irritating, high-pitched laugh of his. "Actually, Blue, ya may be right. I heard it said that this Cooper fella wiped out a whole family from across the Sabine several years back. He'd probably be fun to tangle with!"

"You are all fools!" Blue bellowed.

Fast Bledsoe turned cold. "Ya been ridin' with us over a month, Blue. And ya said you wanted that six thousand as bad as any of us. If you don't like the way we work, do somethin' about it! No half-breed is gonna talk to me that way." He squared up to the Blue Indian, hand hovering over his Colt.

"Sorry," Blue muttered finally. If it weren't for that six-gun on the conceited Fast kid, he'd get him right now, he told himself as he turned to Rodel. "Somebody might've heard your shot and decide to come nosin' around, Zed! What the devil do we do now?"

Rodel waved his hands for quiet. "Let's all calm down, hear? Fast, you gonna be all right in a fight?" He motioned to the wound the cur had given him.

The young man shook his arm limber then drew with amazing speed and dexterity. "Oh, yeah!" He grinned crookedly and returned the gun to its holster with a twirl. "I kept the dog from gettin' too good a hold. I'm ready for action! I could go against Wes

Hardin or Bill Hickok. Ain't none of 'em got nothin' on me!"

Zed could not help but smile as he directed, "Go over to the other cabin and wait. Me and Blue'll stay here with Miguel, then converge on the stage when it arrives. Anybody pops in unexpected like, we'll handle 'em just like we will those with the coach."

"Mi Dios." Miguel groaned, holding his paunch with a bloody hand and trying to find a position on the couch that would be more comfortable. "It hurts badly!"

On his way to get some healing herbs from his gear at the barn, along with the whiskey Zed told him was in the crib, Blue retrieved his knife and whispered to the other two, "Ain't gonna do the Mex no good. By tomorrow night he'll likely be dead or wishin' he was."

Rodel only shrugged as Bledsoe followed the Indian out, then sat down to eat as if the room wasn't filled with carnage. Miguel's moaning nagged at his nerves and he thought perhaps he would let Blue finish him off later on. True, the wound very likely would only worsen, and quickly in this sweltering weather. A man in his shape could do little for the gang's good fortune.

Zed grunted to himself between bites. It was ironic; Miguel Fuantez was going to get whiskey in his guts after all. Just not delivered the way he'd wanted it!

Chapter Two

Never right on time, the bearded stagecoach driver guided the lathered team and vehicle up in front of Tom Cooper's house ten minutes past twelve. The four big horses were spent by the speedy journey from the last station across the ferry on the Sabine, and the driver, Philo, the sprig of a shotgun guard, and the single passenger were all needing to stretch their legs and ease their jolted backs. Some of the fine lunch Mrs. Cooper would have on hand would also be pleasant.

The coach swayed to a halt amid a cloud of dust, and Philo applied the brake as he loosed a gob of tobacco spit. Funny—no one had hurried out at the noise of their approach. Young Stan nearly always showed eagerness in helping change teams and seeing who was riding in the heavy vehicle. Still, although these ideas played at the fringes of Philo's mind, he never expected what came next . . .

Zed Rodel! The tired old driver recognized the weathered face from the likeness on wanted posters in both Texas and Louisiana.

Rodel appeared from the kitchen with a repeater as Philo and the shotgun man were attempting to disembark from the high seat. Philo gave a warning shout before dropping quickly to the ground.

Startled, the other stage employee froze for a second and was caught with two slugs—one from Rodel's Winchester and another from the .52 Sharps belonging to Choctaw Blue, who stepped around the corner of the cabin. The young guard grunted and slumped forward, landing amongst the hind legs of the wheelers and increasing the entire team's fright. Blue ran to the lead animals to keep them from bolting, his single-shot carbine discarded and his Smith & Wesson Russian in hand.

Philo ran back toward the rear of the coach with his drawn revolver, the horses and stage itself shielding him from the Indian and Rodel's guns. The hard voice of the latter bellowed for somebody to get the driver as he levered .44's into the passenger compartment. Philo jerked open the door on the near side and was almost knocked down by the gray-suited drummer escaping the slugs ripping through the heavy carriage.

The stage was beginning to move at the horses' lunges, despite the engaged brake and Blue's efforts to check them.

Crouched low under the coach Philo sent a ball from his old Navy in the direction of the house, then commanded the drummer, "Run for it, man!"

With a big smile on his face, Fast Bledsoe made his appearance in the foray then, having moved up on the quarry's rear from the adjacent cabin, and so cut off the two's retreat with blazing six-shooter. He stood just fifteen paces distant, and his first shot laid the driver out flat, the next two spinning the man in the suit from beneath his silk bowler hat. Bledsoe called out that all was clear to his companions and walked carefully toward the fallen men. The salesman made the mistake of moaning and moving slightly, and the gunman methodically put another bullet right between his long sideburns.

The team was soon unhitched to charge away from the bloody scene, and Bledsoe was jubilant as he and the other two got down and broke open the express box to examine the contents of four bags marked WELLS FARGO. Greenbacks and coins. And lots of them!

"Hot damn!" the kid gunman exclaimed.

Blue concurred his enthusiasm with a vulgar epithet. Rodel was happy but very cool as he deftly went through the two sacks of mail and the drummer's carpetbag for anything else of value. He told the other two to go get their mounts.

"There's some good-lookin' plugs in that barn with ours," Blue said before leaving with Bledsoe.

"Not this time," returned Zed. "More hooves leave more sign, and besides, six thousand can buy lots of good horses if we want 'em."

The other two agreed, and Bledsoe questioned, "Want Miguel's, too? I'm like the Injun—that Mex ain't gonna make it long with holes in his entrails. That wench forked him like a burnt steak!"

"He swears he can sit a saddle." Zed Rodel shrugged while surmising, "When he gets to be too much of a liability, we'll lose 'im. For now, let's just all skin outta here."

Midafternoon found Tom Cooper and Jonas Bretton rocking on the wagon seat, nearing the Circle C under the steady power of the two farm mules. Soft white clouds passed across the strip of blue sky over the timber-lined road. The creaking of the wagon and the rattling of trace chains were not irritating noises to Tom, and if it hadn't been so hot and not for casual conversation, the hardy sandy-haired man might have dozed while loosely holding the lines.

It had been a pleasant day—Tom had sold a load of fresh vegetables and, with the funds received, filled the wagon with enough supplies to see his place well into the winter. And he'd bought a special gift for his wife and son each. Things were going well this year, and had been looking up for the last two.

Likewise Jonas had enjoyed the trip to town to see his betrothed, Ruth Camble. Considering what he had lived through in earlier times of his life, working now for the Coopers seemed like heaven. The future appeared promising, too.

"Stan's sure gonna love that 28 gauge," he predicted.

Tom looked at the black man who was his friend as well as employee. "I learned from Pa up in Ohio that a boy's never too young to know and respect guns. I'll start 'im off bird- and squirrel-hunting with it, stay right with 'im.

"I reckon before ya know it after the weddin' Ruth will have you some young'uns running 'round. Picked ya a good woman, you did, just like my Bell." Cooper had lost much of his Yankee accent during the years in the South, and, for the most part, they had been fine years. Especially those with Bell. He smiled and snapped the lines in his left hand to keep the near mule from shirking his part of the load.

Bretton chuckled. "I reckon you'se right on both counts."

Then they were in view of the homestead, and their good feelings shattered. Tom raced the wagon along the remainder of the shady lane and up to the horseless coach and sprawled bodies, jumped down, and charged into the house, spurs ringing in echo of his pounding footsteps. Jonas Bretton got down slower, '73 Winchester rifle in hand and a numbness in his being.

In the kitchen the sight shocked and sickened Cooper as much or more than the carnage he'd been witness to in the siege of Mobile, Alabama, where both his brother and best friend had met their demise in the War. Stepping over his faithful stock dog, he went to Stan, then Bell. Finding them both cold and chalky white made his eyes burn, but no tears came. Seconds ticked into minutes, and he just stared. A light step behind him made Tom turn to see Jonas taking everything in.

The hired man slowly met his sad eyes and offered feebly, "Lord, I'm sorry, Tom." Then: "Philo's alive, but ya better hurry if you wantta talk to 'im."

Cooper was led to the dying driver propped against the back left wheel of the coach in the shade of the latter. The wounded man's eyes strained to focus on the two squatted before him, and his voice was a whisper. "They was after . . . the money we was carryin'. They . . . got it. Gunned us all. I played possum till they left. Just wanted to make it . . . till somebody . . . showed up."

"Who was it, Philo?" Cooper demanded. "Did ya recognize 'em?"

Philo winced upon taking air into a damaged chest. "It . . . it was Zed Rodel. Didn't know the snake was in these parts." He coughed and his chest rattled ominously. "Water."

Bretton rushed to the well at the far end of the porch. Yet Philo was beyond the need for water or anything else save an undertaker by the time he returned with a brimming gourd dipper. Jonas slung the water into the dust with a hiss. Tom reached over and closed the man's vacant eyes.

He stood slowly and told Jonas, "Help me bury Bell and Stan, then you ride for the sheriff."

Jonas nodded but prophesied, "That big-bellied politician won't know what to do, Tom."

He knew Jonas spoke the truth about the clown who'd been elected to this jurisdiction, a new county made up of parts of two larger ones, with Maple Springs as its seat. "I know. But you'll do it so no one can say we didn't. I'll go ahead and strike the killers' trail."

Jonas didn't argue with his friend and boss, yet he didn't like the hard look that had replaced the previous one of dismay. In silence, because there was nothing he could say to improve the situation, he went to work digging graves near those of Bell's parents. He said a prayer for Cooper while doing so, for he could well imagine what the man was going through, preparing the bodies of his cherished family members.

Indeed Thomas Cooper was devastated, and he washed and dressed his wife and son with careful hands. The country around was more populated than it had been when he entered it and Bell's life six years ago, and for sure there were some neighbor women who would have done this heart-wrenching thing for him. However, Tom wanted it over quickly.

Not out of disrespect for Bell and Stanly, but because of the fire that burned inside him to get hold of their killers. He looked down at the pale faces of his wife and son and that fire only increased. Tenderly, he kissed each before wrapping their bodies in quilts Bell and her mother had made, then mentally vowed, *I'll make this right; I'll get those who did this.*

Jonas stood with him for several minutes before covering them with the freshly turned red soil, each man holding their hats and neither sure of what to say. A slight sighing in the loblolly pines and chirping of katydids were all there was to be heard. They were Christians, but they still didn't know how to appropriately express themselves, and evening wore on but the East Texas day was yet oppressive with heat.

Abruptly Cooper took a folded length of blue-and-pink calico from the quantity of purchased supplies and laid it in the grave with Bell. Upon seeing Bretton looking wonderingly at the colorful material, Tom explained, "I meant to surprise her with that to make a little quilt. You know how she liked to sew. . . . Two days ago she told me she was pregnant, Jonas." Still tears would not come.

Yet the black man had to hold them in check, for he felt true pain for his white friend. Tom laid the new single-barrel shotgun in the grave by his son. Finally, after a respectful, soul-racking silence, the dirt was filled in and a pair of stick crosses were put up until nicer markers could be erected.

From the evidence found in and outside the house, there were four outlaws in all to be caught, and one was wounded with a cooking fork. Bell must have fought back, bless her.

The trio of dead from the stage were laid out in the bedrooms of the Cooper home, Josie's corpse was taken outside and covered in a shallow depression, and things readied for Jonas and Tom to ride in different directions. Less than an hour of daylight was left to burn when they faced each other before mounting. An intense soberness was in their eyes.

"Their trail is clear to the southwest, but I reckon it'll be harder to cut the further they go. I won't leave it if it goes through fire and brimstone," Cooper stated, swinging into the leather.

Bretton fumbled with the bridle reins of his animal. "Leave a good trail yourself. 'Cause I'll try to bring ya help."

Cooper nodded and spurred away at a lope. "Be careful, Tom!" called Jonas suddenly, but the other gave no indication of having heard. The man had plenty on his mind.

Jonas worried over him as he climbed onto his gray mare and struck out for town the quickest way, cross country, ignoring the meandering wagon route with homesteads scattered along at wide intervals. Fortunately, the criminals hadn't bothered the work stock at the homestead, and Jonas was to make sure someone saw after them should he and Cooper be absent long with a posse.

Jonas didn't like the ominous feeling he had. *Lord, how can a good day turn so bad?* He shook his head at the thought; he'd seen it happen before, just not to this extent.

The bandits' trail continued to be fairly plain—Rodel's bunch was obviously going at a rapid clip, more concerned with covering distance than hiding their sign—and it was nightfall that caused Cooper to halt finally. He fixed no supper, only coffee, and built and smoked one cigarette right after the other. Somehow it didn't seem real, the tragedy which had befallen his family. The memories of the awful day kept replaying themselves with vividness, however.

Although they hadn't been married but six years, he and Bell had seen multitudes of good and bad times. They had made a life together with the help of her parents, the Peterses, and a Caddo Indian who'd given his life for them and whose namesake had been Tom's son. There had been plenty of toil and love. Weeks of too much water and those of not enough. The death of Shane, Bell's pa, three years ago from a worn-out body had soon been followed by his wife Martha's death, both having had to depend on their daughter and son-in-law the last few months of their lives.

Tom and Bell had overcome it all to carve a combination ranch, farm, and ultimately stage station from this piece of Texas forest. Only two weeks ago the Coopers had gone to a dance and supper at a neighbor's with Bretton and Ruth, which was thrown to celebrate the bountiful growing season . . . so much fun! In his mind's eye, Tom could see the smiles on Bell's and Stanly's faces. He could almost feel Bell's soft, graceful body against him as they glided over the floor in a waltz.

When the little fire under the coffeepot sputtered out it seemed to Tom his spirit would also. His insides felt hollow, plumb down to the soul. Finally, the tears came. He held his head in his hands and wept harder than he had since the War.

That life at the Circle C for him was over; he lived only to repay the notorious Zed Rodel and his gang for their evil deeds, and he prayed Jonas could get some help from the gutless, money-grubbing county law.

It was late before Cooper lay back on his blankets. Even then he could not sleep in the muggy night.

The place he'd chosen to camp was surrounded by bushy yaupon and Spanish-mulberry thickets that offered concealment and a natural alarm system of noise should anyone approach. His .56 Spencer lay reassuringly nearby, and the converted Army Colt's walnut grip was cool and smooth against his palm, the same .44 that had killed several men, but which he hadn't used in combat with another human in over six years.

The last tracks he'd seen were around seven hours old, and he meant to close that gap some the following day astride his strong black mustang.

Chapter Three

Maple Springs was anything but a wild, bustling place. Save for a mite of activity at the two saloons, all was very quiet by the time Jonas rode up at ten o'clock that night and got down at the new building which served as courthouse and jail. He disturbed a bony fellow nodding off at the desk upon barging in and demanding to see his superior. Deputy Ralph Hinkle unfolded his bean-pole frame to its full six feet, and with irritation said the sheriff had already left for the day and he could take care of any pressing matters himself.

"I don't think so," Bretton stated, and exited.

Sheriff Eli Tooney was a man of habit who liked worldly things, retiring each night after taking the evening meal at his favorite town eatery, to his two-story frame house at the north end of town for a nip of his special stock of bourbon then bed. Being a bachelor had its disadvantages as well as advantages.

Concerned more than anything with money and power, Tooney had done nothing which could be considered training for a lawman while working in a store his whole life, and it had really surprised him to win the first county election after only recently moving here and opening his own mercantile. He'd made many huge promises to help the infant county grow and prosper in safety upon running for the position on an egotistical whim. Seldom did he wear a gun, and thus far had only been forced to catch one rustler of low caliber and jail a couple of disorderly drunks. Nothing remotely life-threatening.

Indeed it was a tame community. Of late, though, he'd begun to worry about the riffraff the planned railroad spur might bring in. . . . Nevertheless, he liked the feeling the tin star gave him.

An urgent banging on the front door brought Tooney from a sound sleep and his cozy fourposter. He looked at the big clock downstairs in the parlor while slipping trousers up over his ample gut under a long nightshirt.

"Hold your horses, I'm comin'." Who the devil would bother him this time of night?

The lamp he lit and held forth illuminated the dark face of a lean but stout black man as Tooney opened the door. "Yeah, what?" The jowly Southerner still had a dislike for the black people who had been free now for over ten years.

Jonas Bretton introduced himself as Tom Cooper's hand out at the Circle C and hurriedly explained everything. Tooney stood dumbfounded.

Zed Rodel! The name chilled his blood. There had been no reports that the bloody outlaw was in the vicinity. Sure, Tooney had wondered at the absence of the stagecoach this Tuesday when notified of it by the fellow on duty at the Wells Fargo office, yet he'd procrastinated about checking into it.

Now the six thousand dollars on the coach was stolen. And five people were dead! But the thing which struck Tooney the hardest was: *This could cost me my badge!*

Jonas said, "You'se the law! What ya gonna do?"

Tooney's mouth worked several times before getting out, "It's pitch dark, man. There's nothing I *can* do!"

"You could be out to the place by first light. Tom's by hisself on their trail, and he may have troubles!"

Eli Tooney did not like this hired man advising him. "I'll send Ralph and some more guys out there for the coach and bodies at dawn."

"And what'll *you* be doin'?" Jonas got a mental picture of the fat man cowering in his office. He'd have liked to have told this bloated skunk just what he thought of him.

Tooney's nerves were set further on edge by the question because he wasn't at all sure of the answer. He sought for a respectable reply, one which wouldn't hint at his terror of a criminal of Rodel's status.

Finally he said with as much assertiveness as he could muster, "Since the town council hasn't seen fit to appoint a marshal, I think it best I remain here to keep the peace. Rodel and the others are likely well out of the country, anyway. I'll wire the Texas Rangers, and I'm positive they can see to this better than lawmen who're confined to small jurisdictions."

Tooney puffed out his thick chest as he gained confidence. "The safety of everyone is my top priority, and of course I'll have to get word to the neighboring counties. I'll—"

Bretton cut him off with one of his rare explosions of temper. "Think, man! What 'bout Tom till the nearest Ranger gets here? They's still gettin' reorganized from the years the State Police was in power!" Bell had been nice enough to teach him to read books and newspapers, and he knew this skunk's words for just what they were—excuses to keep himself in town so he could safely swagger when he ought to be out hunting these badmen.

Flabby jowls quivering with nervous rage, Tooney surmised, "It's a terrible thing, what's happened to the

Coopers. But you've reported it, and that's all ya have the right and obligation to do! I suggest ya catch up to your boss and tell 'im it's in the law's hands, now."

Had Jonas been one to tote a hogleg, right then he would have been sorely tempted to use it to irrigate this self-important man's giant paunch. As it was, the black man had never fired a handgun. And besides, it would only serve to get a mob with a hanging rope on his trail.

"Some law!" he blurted. "You'se jes' washed yo hands of it!"

One of Tooney's pudgy fingers pointed at Bretton. "Listen, boy, if you don't move on, I'll throw ya in a cell for disturbing the peace!"

The wiry black man clenched his fists and teeth at the door that slammed in his face. After a moment of standing there rigidly, breathing fast and short, he turned on his heel and went to his gray mare. In the saddle he trotted down the single, shadowy street to dismount and enter the stage depot and Wells Fargo office to tell the man on duty at the telegraph key what had become of the stage. The fellow in the green eyeshade shook his head vigorously and made a derogatory comment about Sheriff Tooney's lax behavior; the Wells Fargo head men, along with a lot of other people, were not going to be pleased. Jonas said someone would need to go out and see to the station work at the Circle C until further notice—stock was out there, too, for the stage company and the homestead's work animals. The Wells Fargo employee swore it all would be seen to.

Again on the mare, Jonas guided her past the bank next door and into a break in the false-fronted buildings by Grinder's Café. There in the dark alleyway, he dismounted and climbed the stairs to Ruth Camble's rented room above the eatery. He knocked three times before hearing light footsteps and the cautious demand, "Who's there?"

"It's Jonas. Open up, darlin', I'se gotta talk to ya."

A light began to glow inside, and the comely woman who was to be his bride this fall admitted him with a half-stern, half-worried look. "What's the matter with you, Jonas Bretton, callin' on me in the dead of night?" She pulled her robe snugly around her.

"It ain't good." Bretton spilled the story to her, and likewise poured out the silent tears he hadn't shown Tom. Ruth was as devastated as her fiancé; the Coopers were noble folks, and she'd looked forward to joining Jonas and them out on the Circle C in autumn. Many a plan had been made.

She gripped Jonas's arm and said, "That's awful." She shook her head. "And what a fine sheriff we've got, good for nothin' but eating and struttin' around like an ol' rooster!"

Bretton wiped his face with a bandanna and felt like a fool. "Just wanted to let ya know I'm riding after

Tom. Ruth, the look I saw in his eyes tells me he'll not let it drop. Not that I can blame 'im. Rodel could be long gone befo' a Ranger gets here." He paused and she knew what was coming next before he said it. "I'll follow 'im, whatever he decides to do."

"Please be careful." Her voice was an urgent whisper.

He kissed her velvet lips firmly, his work-hardened hands holding her unblemished, chocolate-brown neck as the kiss lingered. Pulling back, he spoke huskily, "I been around some and worked fo' lots of men since leavin' that plantation on the Trinity after the War. Ya gets to know a fella pretty good by laborin' with 'im ever' day, and Tom Cooper's the best of the lot, friend as well as boss.

"You know as good as me how black folk is treated by most, even a lot of those what fought fo' the North. But the Coopers ain't never had no qualms 'bout skin color. Wasn't nothing I wouldn't have done fo' Tom, Bell, and Stanly. And I believe they'd have done the same by me.

"I gotta stand by Tom, now more'n ever. Keep 'im from getting into troubles. A fella can get reckless under the circumstances he's under."

With closed eyes Ruth nodded, curly black hair bobbing on her shoulders. She understood his loyalty. Although she wanted to keep him near her and away from any fight, it wouldn't have been right to ask him not to go. So she met his solid gaze and repeated her request for him to be careful.

"I will." Another kiss, this one much shorter, and he was out, down the steps, and away at a gallop on his bronc.

Ruth locked the door and braced her back against it. "Jesus, help 'em both," she prayed.

Rodel was in a bad mood the next morning. Neither he, Blue, nor Bledsoe had managed much rest during the night hours because of Miguel Fuantez. The Mexican, in his agony and fear, hadn't fallen asleep until just a while ago. Sick of his moaning and complaining, and now sure he would soon die of his wound, the trio had slipped out in the dark hour before dawn. They needed to be away, and Miguel wouldn't be alone long—he'd be in hell.

Two miles further west, with first light tingeing the sky behind them, the riders' squeaking saddle leather and jingling bit chains added to the sounds of wild creatures awakening. Choctaw Blue's cigarette glowed as he dragged before saying around it, "We're better off without the Mex."

Fast Bledsoe concurred, "Yeah, no sense in lettin' his misfortune cause us to get caught. Did he really think we'd chance getting him to a doc? Begged us all night long!"

In the lead, Zed only grunted. A small part of him

felt sympathy for the Mexican; Miguel had ridden with him longer than the other two. However, Rodel was a calloused, practical man, and his bad feeling for one of his gang would not cause him to jeopardize his own hide. Should he be apprehended, it was sure no court would sentence him to anything save a quick meeting with a hangman atop a scaffold before the public.

And that wasn't acceptable to the outlaw leader. Not at all.

He guided his big chestnut stallion into maneuvers aimed at throwing kinks in their trail. "Won't be too long 'fore we split up. Aw, there's a good many miles to cover, but we'll move quick." In spite of the rugged vastness of Rodel's range of thieving, there were lots of offbeaten paths etched in his mind from past use. He grinned. "And I reckon we can get by on provisions acquired from obligin' farmers."

Bledsoe chuckled. "I figure another day or two of the Injun's cookin', and I'll have a big hankering for some more vittles fixed by the fair sex."

Zed made a lewd remark. No less dangerous than the other two, Blue kept his Missouri trotter along at the rear of the procession and wondered again at his decision to fall in with these fellows who didn't hesitate to treat women with the same brutality as men.

He told himself not to worry, though. At least they were traveling in stealth now, and Blue was no stranger to violence, starting at age sixteen when he slit the throat of a pompous keelboat captain who called him a dirty breed. Since then he'd done as he pleased to get by, and now told himself as long as he wasn't caught, hurting women could be just as profitable as men.

And this Indian did not plan on getting caught. So why not? After what lay behind them, he was in too deep to get out now, anyway. Also, his share of the take from the coach helped to persuade Blue that Rodel's operations were worthwhile.

The first thing Miguel Fuantez noticed upon coming to was that it was full daylight. Then, with shocking clarity, he saw that he was alone. The tiny clearing was void of everything but him, his gear, and horse. Staring at the latter tied so close yet so far away, Miguel began calling out for his *compañeros* in a hoarse voice which belied his fear and became steadily weaker.

After straining to rise and go for his horse, he made only two steps before his legs buckled beneath him. He lay on his side in a fetal position, hands clasped on his swollen belly, a searing pain inside. It was thirty minutes he lay there sweating, hurting, and hissing Spanish curses at the *hombres* who'd abandoned him before he mustered the strength to crawl over and pull himself into a slumped position against a post oak.

His eyes went back to his blankets and other things

as he panted like a dog. His mouth and throat were parched. He was feverish and he knew that he was bleeding internally.

Merciful God, why didn't they kill me in my sleep instead of leaving me here like this? The bandit was close to tears, for he was sure, even if he reached his mount, he would not be able to pull up and stay aboard its bare back. It was doubtful he could even do it if someone were there to saddle and bridle the animal for him.

Miguel looked from his canteen to the holstered Dragoon over there with his belongings. Maybe . . .

It doesn't take a brave man to be evil, and he cried like a baby. The pain in his inflamed bowels was intense, but he feared death. He was not at all sure he could pull the trigger of that cap-and-ball revolver to end it himself should he manage to crawl back to his bed and gear.

Chapter Four

Soon as he could see the ground, Cooper was on the trail. It was more difficult to read for there had been a heavy dew, and the quarry's prints were also frequently obliterated by mats of dead leaves and pine needles. Several miles west and south of the winding road to Maple Springs from Louisiana, Tom rode relentlessly, observant of everything and keeping his thoughts on what he was doing as much as he could. It was hard, because a distressed man's mind will wander to every angle of whatever is distressing him.

Once he lost the path of the single-file riders entirely in an open stretch of piney woods for close to a half-hour. A few broken wood ferns and a partial hoofprint got him back on the right track after many ever-widening circles. Rodel and his cronies were going

36

due west now, keeping well away from human habitation, and, although Tom Cooper was no amateur at reading sign, he wished for the dead Josie.

The brindle cur had been a good, all-around dog. She worked hogs and cows alongside Tom and Jonas, never hesitating at waterway, dense chaparral, or vicious animal, doing whatever was asked of her no matter the implied danger. Too, she could be set on the scent of anything else, wild or tame, and be depended on to find it. Thus Cooper knew the cur he and his father-in-law had trained from a pup would have increased the speed of his present hunt.

About midmorning Cooper checked the black gelding at the crest of a magnolia ridge and shucked his carbine from its boot. He sniffed the air and nodded. Charred wood, no longer burning, yet recently so. Last night most likely.

Already the early-day coolness was gone, and the man's shirt clung damply to him as he stepped down and tethered the black. Sweat ran among the sandy hairs of his beard and caused dust and grime to stick to it, much as it did to the raven coat of the mustang.

Tom removed his spurs, put them in the saddlebags, and left the animal with a pat on the neck. The building heat was quickly evaporating the night's dew, and Tom walked slowly to lower the amount of noise his steps made on the forest litter. Scanning the terrain, he crept into a scant breeze, listening for voices or movement, his Spencer at the ready.

Off the ridge he traversed a brush-choked baygall dotted with puddles which only disappeared in prolonged dry spells. Horse tracks could be seen here and there, also a place where they squeezed through some mayhaws and tupelo gums wound thoroughly with blooming Virginia creeper. Beyond this depression the earth rose again, yet more gently. Tom remained cautious, tense, while steadily moving ahead.

A sudden racket erupted on his left and he wheeled with the carbine's butt firmly against his shoulder. Just a durned swamp rabbit busting into a briar patch! Cooper stifled a nervous oath and slowly lowered the cocked hammer.

The snort of a horse pulled his attention back the way he had been going. Someone was in that thicket yonder. Still careful but very eager, he started on.

Concealed at the edge of the small opening, he studied the camp therein. Obviously more had been there, yet just one man and bronc occupied it now, and Tom had to watch for several seconds to see the faint breathing of the Mexican slouched against the post oak. He looked near death, his shirt stained dark with blood above the belt line, his sombrero lying at his side.

Cooper skirted the clearing and found Rodel and the others' sign leading on west. Tom estimated the age of the tracks before striding confidently toward the un-conscious Mexican. He had the huge bore of his long gun in Miguel's face when the latter's eyes fluttered open.

Brain clouded with fever, Miguel focused on the gun and the hard face of its wielder. "*Por favor . . .* I need help."

Cooper spoke through clenched teeth, "Like my wife and boy needed help with you and those other devils, huh?" He saw fear develop in the other by his expression and faster breathing. "Tell me where the others headed, and do it quick!"

Miguel stuttered, "They l-left me, *Señor*. I . . . I must s-see a *medico*. Please!" he whined in English, terrified now at the look of Cooper, husband and father to the dead woman and child.

"Blast you, tell me where y'all were plannin' to go! I want to know who the other two with Rodel are." He cared not what this pathetic beast's name was, for Tom wasn't about to put him up a marker when he was through with him.

The Mexican tried to beg help once more and Coo-per made him gasp with a kick to his inflamed mid-section. "By God, you tell me what I want to hear, or I'll turn ya every way but loose!"

Miguel owed nothing to those who'd left him for dead, and after recovering from the impact of Cooper's boot toe, he began, "One ees a breed . . . called Choctaw Blue. The other one, he ees just a *muchacho*. His name is Luke Bledsoe—they c-call heem Fast . . . 'cause of his speed weeth a *pistola*."

He grimaced at the pain in his ruined intestines upon taking a deep breath. This was the only way he could spite those motherless dogs he'd once rode with, and so he continued, "We were goin' to split up near one of Zed's hideouts on the Neches Reever. He and Blue, they weel go on to the shack in the bottom. Fast said . . . he said he would go into a town called Malloy for while. I was . . . goin' to go there weeth him. I swear . . . that ees all, *Señor*!"

Cooper stared down at this man he hated, wanting to ask about Bell and Stan's last few minutes but afraid to at the same time. It had been disturbing enough to see their lifeless bodies, and to hear the details of their deaths would just hurt him more.

Instead of saying anything, with a cruelness never before a part of Tom, he kicked the man viciously twice more. He watched him double over and fall sideways, then heard Jonas Bretton's shout from back in the direction of his tied mustang.

"Tom, you'se all right? Where ya at?"

"Fine! Across the flat! Ride on in and bring my horse!" Tom hoped Jonas had the sheriff with him, yet doubted it.

That doubt was confirmed when Jonas trotted up alone. The black man looked tired as he related everything Tooney had said, then: "Changed mounts and got on yo trail at first light." He dismounted to allow the lathered sorrel with the Circle-C brand some rest. The animal had been used hard since leaving the homestead early that morning when Jonas took her and put up his personal gray, and the normal light hue of her blond color was now darkened by sweat.

Cooper's knuckles went white at the thought of their spineless sheriff, and he murmured harshly, "Figured such of Tooney! Thanks, though," then told Jonas what he had learned from the collapsed Mexican.

"He still alive?" queried Jonas, peering at the motionless form by the tree.

Tom retrieved the coiled lasso from the saddle on his black which Bretton held with the sorrel. "Not for long, he ain't."

"Tom"—Jonas swallowed hard—"you can't jes' hang 'im."

The retort to his friend was unusually rough. "Just watch me!"

Although Bretton was every bit the hard-built man Cooper was, even younger by five years, he didn't obstruct Tom's path as he went to the dying man, shaking out a loop in the rope. Never had Jonas seen him this way, not that he couldn't understand the white man's feelings, and he stood with uncertainty as Tom tossed the straight end of the lariat over one of the post oak's strongest limbs.

"Let's take 'im in, Tom. Let a judge order this."

Cooper wheeled on him with vehement words. "How can ya say that? I won't lose time in gettin' those other vermin by doing everything by the law's book! That law ain't doin' its job, and I'll just have to do things my way! If it was *your* wife and boy, you'd sure feel different!"

Bretton looked at the ground, a sense of failing his friend and employer strong within him. He said nothing. What could he say to defend himself that wouldn't make him seem a traitor to this man and his murdered family?

Cooper stooped over to put the loop around Miguel's stubby neck. Abruptly he cursed and dropped the outlaw's dark head with disgust. Rising, he turned and started recoiling the lariat.

"Your weak stomach will be happy. He's already dead," he announced sarcastically.

Jonas fumbled with the reins of the blond mare while Tom set free the criminal's picketed horse with a slap on the rump. Bretton's mind was spinning enough already when he was directed, "Go home, Jonas. See to the place. I'm goin' after Rodel and the other two."

"No, I go with ya." It was the first time ever Bretton had straight-out refused one of Cooper's orders. "Somebody'll watch after the Circle C, I made sure of that, and you need help."

Tom Cooper's breathing had slowed, but it was still shallow. And his tone was terse after he tightened the cinch on his mustang. "I reckon you're more suited to nurse animals and crops than what I'll be doing. Besides, no tellin' how long I'll be gone."

Bretton's pride was scorched by the first statement. Yet he kept from bristling and only surmised levelly as Cooper swung up, "It's sho 'nough true that I'm no fightin' man. But I can shoot this new Winchester plenty straight, and I wantta ride with ya, Tom."

The logical part of Tom Cooper wanted Jonas with him, knew he was a dependable companion, but the anger and pain to the forefront of his soul made him surly. So his response cut like a double-edged knife. "Then you hear this: I aim to catch and hang all that were involved in my family's killing, unless they force me to plug 'em first. Either way, they'll die.

"If you're with me, you'll do as I say and make no comment about it." He paused just long enough to give what came next more emphasis. "Or you'll draw what you have coming from the Circle C and hightail it!"

Bretton nodded and hurried to mount and follow the gelding which was booted away at a canter. The blond sorrel stood over two hands higher than the mustang and was of thoroughbred blood, yet she was not held back in order to match pace with the hardy cayuse Tom had owned so long, caught wild on the Brazos and sold to him in Louisiana. The little black horse stepped lively. Jonas stayed to Tom's rear and held his peace; the atmosphere between them was sufficient hint to not attempt conversation.

All was easy concerning reading sign, until three miles later when the trail dropped into a steep-banked stream with not much more than an inch of water running over a bottom of white sand. Tracks did not ascend the opposite bank, and enough time had elapsed for the current to have demolished all but the most distinct impressions in the soft bottom. With none evident for the first few yards both up and down the narrow stream bed, Cooper curtly sent Jonas up it to the north and west while he went along the meandering rivulets toward the opposing point of the compass.

Cooper could deal with his fierce emotions best by keeping his mind steadily on the hunt, so he studied the surroundings intently for any clue to the quarry's passing. The branch wound down through hills covered in giant pines and into hardwood bottoms, most of the time the banks so close together Cooper's stirrups were only inches from rubbing the vertical walls on either side as high as the pommel. In the lower breaks, switch cane and chaparral grew so dense in a grayish-green mass on the lips of the arroyo that the heat was sweltering. A breeze wanted to blow but it was high and couldn't make up its mind to really get started, so down here in the brush all was still and muggy.

The sandy-haired man wiped some of the grime from his face and neck and squinted at a broken willow sapling which had grown slanting out across the wash. Hope increased. Ten yards on and there was half of a horseshoe outline in some damp sand above the shallow water level; a bit further some horse droppings tainted the clear water of the branch. Cooper walked the gelding along and rested his right hand on his thigh near the tied-down Colt, despite the unlikeliness of an ambush.

A spattering of distorted prints showed where a small number of riders had scrambled up a cut in the right side around a westward curve in the stream. Tom went far enough to see the sign was rather good from there on, and then turned to lope back for Jonas.

Strange how men could be so evil to others of their own species just for self-gain. Cooper wasn't a stranger to trouble, but things had been so good and natural these last years! Of course there had been hard work, worry, and a bit of heartache through the life on the homestead, but what person had absolutely none of that? Yet, oh, the happiness!

Now it was gone, every bit of it. And it rankled.

Tom grimaced at the crumbling of the wall he'd put up to shut off the sorrow from his consciousness. He forced his thoughts back to physical action, hunting

Zed Rodel—a man who until yesterday had been no more than the name of a notorious bandit to the Coopers—and making him pay.

Bretton's whipcord form rocked rhythmically in the saddle from years of experience at doing such in stock-raising jobs. Likewise from sodbusting, although he wasn't a giant, his muscles had developed into the ripples of a man used to work and lots of it. By his easy appearance, riding and looking, one could not know the turmoil in his own mind and heart.

Bell and young Stan's murders had not only affected Tom. There was a nagging inside Jonas that wanted revenge, too. The Good Book said, "An eye for an eye and a tooth for a tooth." But civilized law had codes and ethics which often slowed and hindered the punishment of outlaws, and generally they were at odds with the quick justice the common man wanted.

Jonas was torn and worried over Tom. Less than these circumstances had destroyed many a good fellow.

Bretton neck-reined the mare up out of the branch and around at Cooper's hasty approach. The mustang snorted after sliding to a stop on a heavy carpet of pine straw.

"We'll rest the horses then move on. I found their trail. It's goin' due south. If we gained any, it's awful little!"

Jonas Bretton complied quietly. Under a loblolly he sat and munched hardtack. Strange for them, the two comrades shared a meal that day without a single, solitary word, and were riding again within the hour.

Chapter Five

Camp was made when visibility of the trail in the dense forest decreased to a point where proceeding would have been counterproductive. Jonas stripped the horses and left them picketed to roll and graze on a grassy knoll, and Tom scraped up the makings of a fire to prepare bacon, biscuits, and coffee. He felt the enemy was still far enough ahead not to see the fire's light or smell the smoke, so he dwelled on what he was doing, then on the day's travel while supper cooked, as he leaned against his saddle smoking a cigarette.

For the most part they had headed straight south after picking up Rodel and the others' trace where it left the shallow arroyo. Roads and paths of human origin were being shunned by the fugitives as they

48

followed game trails or blazed their own, and Cooper could detect nothing to hint that he was gaining on them in the least. In the severe July heat, their horses had to be considered lest they be ridden down. So, likely just matching the outlaws' speed, the latter kept in the lead by more or less the same distance as the day before.

There was the very real possibility the Mexican had lied, Tom determined once again after discarding the butt of his smoke and flipping the sizzling bacon in the skillet. Therefore, it would be risky to start out straight for the Neches River to locate a little town called Malloy that neither he nor Jonas was acquainted with when there was yet good sign to cut.

Absently, Tom rolled and lit another cigarette; it was in idle moments like these that it was the hardest to keep his mind from painful thoughts of Stanly and his mother. Firelight played on the dark, rugged figure of Jonas Bretton sitting across from him, and Tom felt shame for the way he had talked to him earlier. Not a day since beginning work for him and Bell had the man ever shirked or failed a responsibility. A better hand could not have been found whether the task be breaking horses, tending crops, working hogs, or punching cows. And, also, there had been a family-like relationship between the Coopers and Jonas Bretton.

The black man poured cups of hot brew when the

coffee announced its readiness with a loud bubbling. Taking the offered serving, Cooper concluded that the quiet between them was as unacceptable as the guilt he felt for the solemn look on Bretton's ebony countenance.

"Jonas, I apologize for the way I've acted."

"Don't worry 'bout it. You'se under a mighty big strain."

"That I am. But I still had no right to speak to ya the way I did this mornin'."

Bretton dished up the meat and bread on tin plates for them. "I can't say how sorry I am, Tom. Wasn't none better than yo Bell and Stanly. I jes' don't want ya to make a mistake by goin' after these men on yo own. Mebbe the Rangers'll come soon."

Tom washed a bite down with coffee. "Yeah, well, till they do, I'll stomp my own snakes. That don't mean you gotta be in this, though. You got a good woman waitin' on ya."

Jonas met the other man's gaze without flinching. "Ruth knows I'll be with ya till it's over. She sho hated to hear what happened."

A time passed in silence as they ate, Cooper thinking of things which hurt, heartened some by Jonas's friendship. He asked him finally, "What in the world am I gonna do without Bell and Stan? They were everything to me, Jonas, everything."

It was several seconds before Bretton found his

voice. "You got to go on like they'd want ya to. It'll be awful hard, I'll grant that, but I ain't ever seen you give up on anythin'. You'se saddled and rode some mighty tough broncs."

Tears burned Cooper's eyes and his throat tightened. Once Rodel and the rest were made to pay, he just wasn't sure he'd have the strength to live anymore. Determination to punish the gang which had destroyed his life seemed to be the only thing that was keeping him going, and he said as much, then:

"A man lives a good portion of his life to find the right woman for 'im, Jonas. For me, that was Bell. Just a few good years we had, too few . . . now this."

Those words, combined with the tone in which they were spoken, scared Jonas Bretton. He cleared his throat. " 'Bitterness and revenge never helped nobody,' Ma used to tell me back in the slave days. Tom, remember what the Landises done to you when you first came to Texas." He hoped he wouldn't anger Tom by bringing up the story of the past in comparison to this.

Cooper sighed deeply, already feeling the craving of a cigarette since finishing the food. The time his friend spoke of was the last time he'd faced men through clouds of gun smoke.

He stated, "There's a big difference, Jonas. I shot their brother in self-defense, and Rodel and his bunch did what they done out of pure meanness. I didn't want *that* fight; I *do* want this one.

"Rodel and Bledsoe and that Indian will just keep livin' the same till someone puts a stop to 'em. Meanness is in them like the instinct is in a wolf to bring down a spring fawn. There ain't no way to get rid of either, short of death."

Bretton watched him stride off into the brush with his bedroll, pondering the statement that he could find no argument with, and realizing a man sometimes needs to be alone. Tom Cooper was a man who knew well it is not always the other person that trouble comes to, but that fact would make this bad dose no easier for him to swallow. How could it for any fellow who really loved his family?

As he rinsed the cooking and eating wares and put them away, Jonas thought of the times Cooper had spoken of the past and the Indian who had given his life for a man he'd not known long. On several occasions Bretton had seen the Caddo's grave and read its marker.

Taysha, the native word for friend and ally—that was what Jonas must be to Tom more than ever now.

A couple of days later found Rodel and the two left in his small gang drawing up at a secluded little farm west and south of the bustling old town of San Augustine. A gaunt fellow with suspenders holding up dirt-stiffened trousers stopped his heavy draft horse in the field he was preparing for a crop of sweet potatoes to lean on the handles of his plow and watch the trio of riders approach his house.

Zed likewise looked at him across the distance and sent Blue in that direction as a girl with golden curls came onto the porch. "Your mammy home, Miss?" asked Zed, noticing her young attractiveness.

"Yah, sure." She spoke with an accent from somewhere in the Old World.

Fast Bledsoe leered after getting down from his horse. This fresh little thing couldn't be much more than fifteen! He asserted, "That's right good, 'cause we could use some cooking and tending to by some ladies."

The girl was old enough to know these men didn't have good intentions, and she'd begun to back toward the door, ice in her heart, when the redheaded young fellow came for her. Her papa cried out and her eyes went to the field just in time to see the Indian plunge his huge knife into his chest. She bolted inside then, screaming for her mother.

"Get her, Fast," Zed Rodel hissed, charging through the screen door behind the younger man and their comely prey.

Bledsoe caught hold of the girl's faded cotton dress just as she gained a spacious kitchen from the scantily furnished parlor. Suddenly an older and more filled-out version of the lass appeared from a side room with a fully cocked scattergun. Rodel saw the twin bores gaping at him as they swung his way, and he dove clear as the first blast sounded.

The range was so close the charge of squirrelshot didn't spread much as it swarmed past the bandit leader and ripped a hole in the plank wall. Fast Bledsoe clutched the girl in the bend of his left arm while the opposite hand flashed for the pistol down low on his hip. Zed was attempting to roll out of line of the enraged mother's 12 gauge when he heard a pair of .44-40 cartridges explode one after the other, and he saw the woman jerk backward to fall dead, sending the second load from the scattergun into the ceiling.

Bledsoe cuffed the hysterical girl lightly on the side of the head with his gunbarrel. "Settle down, Missy!" She did, sobbing, and he holstered the Colt.

Zed's breathing was slowing upon getting to his feet and giving his thanks to the redhead. With the enthusiastic grin that seemed to forever be on his face, Bledsoe told him not to mention it. Then Blue entered wielding his Arkansas toothpick with the immigrant farmer's blood still on it.

"Whew!" was his only comment, low but emphatic.

Rodel became his hard, confident self, saying to the Choctaw, "Don't get yourself in a stew. All's well." It was almost noon, and he took a deep breath to calm himself further and surmise, "We'll keep one on watch all the time and take our ease here a few hours."

Nodding, Bledsoe hugged the girl against her wishes, then released her with the order to behave herself. Choctaw Blue wiped and put away his knife, admitting to himself that he liked the looks of this girl. He indeed figured he'd do all right with Zed—the leader had sense to lead a good operation, had been doing just that for some while now—and it wasn't like Blue was planning to get caught. He'd die first. Since striking the owl-hoot trail he had always vowed that. Surrender wasn't an option to him.

"What's your name, Miss?" drawled Rodel.

The girl stood trembling with head down amid the triangle of outlaws, tears on her cheeks at the terror which had blackened such a normal day. Her voice wavered. "Greta."

"Purty name." The gang leader chuckled and bent forward to see her fearful, emerald eyes. "Well, Greta, you have the honor of playin' hostess to Zed Rodel and his boys." She sobbed as he stepped forward.

Tom and Jonas had had considerable good luck in cutting sign the last two days, and it was an hour before dark when they got to the same secluded farm way off a wagon road at the end of a dim lane lined with beech and hickory trees, quite a distance from where they started this trek and with no indication it would soon end.

What they discovered was a ransacked farmhouse, a murdered couple, and a young woman barely clinging to life. Disgust mounted in them both as they wrapped her unconscious form in blankets. With very little said Bretton rode hard to bring back the first neighbor he could find, and Cooper remained at the beaten girl's side.

Ill at ease about the child's poor condition, it seemed a longer wait to Tom than it actually was. He gave thought to her and her dead folks, his own destroyed family, and what he wanted to do to those men who had done it all.

A portly husband and wife returned at dusk with Jonas. They appeared an upstanding couple of middle age, and quickly aided Tom and Jonas in loading the girl and corpses into their flat-bed farm wagon. Naturally shocked at the tragedy, the man and woman introduced themselves as the Doyles, and said the devastated household was a new family to the community who went by the name of Hadzlot.

Mrs. Doyle claimed, "We thought we heard some shots around dinnertime, but somebody's always out huntin', ya know. Land's sake, what they done to this child!"

"We'll get her into San Augustine to the doc, and I'll notify the sheriff," her husband declared and pulled his heavy body up onto the seat as his wife got in the back with the hurt girl and her dead parents. "You said ya thought it was Zed Rodel?" he made sure.

Jonas let Tom reply, "Gotta be. If the sheriff ain't here by morning, we'll set out by ourselves." Jonas had already told of the reason they came about being here to find this.

Doyle wished them luck and clucked to the team. Cooper and Bretton stood motionless until the wagon had vanished from sight and hearing into the muggy night.

"By the Lord, Tom, you're right! They gotta be stopped. I never seen such cruelty except to slaves."

Cooper flinched at the black man breaking the eerie quiet. There didn't seem to be a creature alive for miles except them. "Maybe we'll get help from the law in this county," Cooper said.

They set up camp at the farm to await dawn and, hopefully, the sheriff. The latter, accompanied by a posse of three, clattered up on blowing horses an hour ahead of sunrise. Jonas and Tom arose from fitful napping to build up the fire and fix coffee and talk things over with the newcomers until good daylight.

Sheriff Dunigan was a rawboned fellow with a crisp, assertive manner. He hunkered by the flames with his cup as if it were cold weather, and let it be known right off in a deeply Southern twang that Cooper and Bretton could join his small group of manhunters, but they would darn well follow his orders. Like with the Hadzlots, Dunigan was sorry about Tom's tragedy and the failure of the Maple Springs law to do its job.

He'd been hearing some about Tooney's lethargic running of justice in the little neighboring county. A wire had come from him several days ago to San Augustine warning of Rodel and vowing the Rangers were going to do something about him.

Dunigan allowed, "If we don't have any luck catchin' the snakes before they get outta my jurisdiction, maybe we'll at least go far enough to help whoever the state law sends by knowing some about the direction they're headed."

Cooper told the bit learned from the dying Mexican, and Dunigan frowned at their not taking the cadaver in to the closest authorities. Tom, he didn't really give a hoot what the gentleman thought. He just heard Dunigan out, along with the names of the three hastily picked possemen, which were almost immediately forgotten, and gave a bob of the head. He was inclined to have his own opinion of the greenness he sensed in these fellows, just yahoos Dunigan found in the saloons with nothing better to do, most likely. Yet he'd tolerate them because they *were* trying, unlike the fat Eli Tooney.

Jonas held his peace, wanting the criminals brought to justice as bad as anyone. He did worry, however, that Tom might get himself in trouble by gunning the men in cold blood if Dunigan apprehended them. Very likely Cooper and the sheriff would come to odds.

And he didn't hold those possemen in high regard as fighting men, either, not like Tom had come to look and act of late. All but the one who was bald, called Tabor, appeared inexperienced and red-eyed, even Dunigan to an extent.

But then who was Jonas Bretton to judge? He was anything but a gunman, himself.

Right then he just wanted to be moving, on the trail of the killers, so hopefully it would be over and his friend could get past this awful time and on with his life. If he could.

Bluebirds searched for a breakfast of insects and worms in the grass and weeds around the fields and outbuildings on the Hadzlot place. Westward led the sign of the desperados, clear and steady; Dunigan insisted on riding at the front of the group. A heavy fog drenched everything, cloaked every hollow and pocket of brush, outlined every ridge. The six men and horses spooked a doe and fawn drinking in the backwater of a creek, and the cavalcade shoved on during a morning which offered little cool air. Not only was it hot, but one could feel moisture in the still, heavy atmosphere.

They came to an abandoned campsite about nine o'clock, and there Cooper stepped down with Dunigan, ignoring the lawman's disapproving glance, to examine the various marks on the ground up close. While the rest swapped comments and theories, he discovered that one plug in the hunted number was in possession of a shoe with a distinctive chip in it, and Tom chided himself for not noticing it sooner. But perhaps it had only recently been damaged. Such as this could sometimes prove helpful. He told the others of his find as they again started west.

"Tracks ain't more'n two or three hours old here," Tabor soon observed, and Cooper mused the man had a good eye.

Before long the terrain they traveled became rich hummocks carpeted in alternating grids of fern, stiff grasses, pine needles, and leaves. The day wore on, the heat getting more oppressive, and on all the forest debris the age of the trail was hard to determine. Just an occasional broken plant or scuff in the ground litter told them they were on the right track at all. Sweat drenched both animals and men, and the former didn't step as lively as just after sunup; some drooped their long heads as they plodded forth. But a rest was vetoed, for everyone believed they must be gaining on their prey, and an imminent rain threatened to wash out the scant sign.

Cooper's gelding wasn't antsy over the rumblings in the gathering clouds. The mustang was extremely gentle and accustomed to loud noises, such as a gunshot from its rider during a hunt, so the sandy-haired man rocked easily with the smooth motion of the horse while scanning everything with his eyes, and at the same time allowing his mind to work on the problem.

Would it rain heavily? Could they catch up to the outlaw trio before it did? Rodel's party evidently wasn't worried about pursuers—they had spent a devilish time at the Hadzlot place, and from the tracks found occasionally now, they weren't pressing themselves.

There was another question, too. Would these men with Tom and Jonas be a help or a hindrance if they did catch up to the murdering thieves?

Tom shook his head at the incessant chattering of the bright-eyed kid in the posse. *Boy like that thinks something such as this is an exciting adventure to prove he's a man! Won't Dunigan ever shut him up?*

The sheriff didn't, but the talk of first one thing then another by the young man had gotten on Jonas's nerves also. "Couldn't slip up on a tame hoss with all this racket," he said with enough inflection to get over his point.

Actually, Dunigan had been conversing *with* the kid off and on that morning, and he, like those in his posse, were taken aback by a rebuke from a black man. "What ya gettin' at, Bretton?" he asked in his lazy Southern speech.

The kid wagged his own noisy tongue. "Yeah, you talkin' smart to us?"

Cooper was opening his mouth to spew the lawman and boy with harsh reprimands when they topped a big rise and it became imperative for everyone's attention to shift to something else. The peak they sat their horses on was anchor for towering longleaf pines and thin, crooked blackjacks. The ground fell away steadily and severely to the Attoyac Bayou bottom, and as the six riders pulled up and looked ahead as one, they saw the white-headed outlaw and his two companions no more than a hundred yards away. In an open pin-oak flat just this side of some dense undergrowth, the hunted trio had been taking the rest Dunigan's posse so much needed.

"Hold it, Rodel!" Dunigan yelled, jerking up his repeater. "This is the San Augustine Sheriff!"

Alerted by voices and other noises of the group's approach before they ever came in sight on the knoll, Rodel, Blue, and Bledsoe were already scrambling for their tethered horses. The sheriff's command had no halting effect on them. Zed was the first in the saddle and levered two shots up at their vantage point, then wheeled to flee with his cohorts in the opposite direction, toward the cover along the bayou.

Although the Winchester balls struck harmlessly short, they were sufficient to make Dunigan's mount sidle and throw his own shot off mark. Tom cocked and fired his Spencer just ahead of swift rifle fire from Bretton and the stern-looking Tabor. Then the horses did become nervous, prancing and side-stepping to different degrees, all save Tom's black, which only lowered its head at the signal of its master rising in the stirrups. Dunigan fought his animal and gave the command for everyone to dismount and shoot straight.

The glory-hunting kid in the posse gave a whoop that would have done a Comanche buck proud and drummed his boot heels on his mount's ribs to charge down the steep grade, Remington six-shooter out of its cross-draw holster and in hand. "Let's get 'em!"

A moment's hesitation, and then the third posseman in the sheriff's original group decided his young comrade had a better, more heroic notion than the lawman—ride the varmints down! So he hit the lowland right behind the boy and his barking pistol.

"Blast you all, come back here!" bleated Dunigan at the insubordinates.

If not for the seriousness of the matter, he would have been a funny sight trying to dismount from his panicking cayuse. While Tabor got down and kept a hold of his mount, Dunigan practically fell off his, releasing it to run off.

Apparently the older of the two who were making the charge either had a change of heart or chose not to defy the shout of the sheriff, because he swung back to the ridge.

Through clenched teeth Tabor said as he fired his

carbine, "That boy'll get his guts shot out down there!"

Tom cursed agreement. He knew enough of fighting to assume the kid was racing to his death; Rodel would likely use the wall of chaparral yonder as a defense line, and on this overlooking promontory was where they could attack the bandits best as they retreated, offering their backs for targets.

Tabor and Sheriff Dunigan both were firing now, the first hindered some by holding his horse. Bretton, off his sorrel mare, worked the action of his long gun again, more deliberately, and saw the Choctaw's animal stumble but keep on, crashing into the thicket ahead and to the right of Bledsoe and Rodel. Since the mustang was giving him no real problems, Cooper paid no heed to Dunigan's order to dismount and concentrated on making sure his next bullet connected with Rodel who brought up the rear.

It did, at least with his hand. The huge .56 slug burned across the knuckles, numbing the member so that the Winchester fell from his grasp.

Zed Rodel's heart was pounding like the hooves of his stallion upon entering the underbrush beyond the pin-oak flat. As always, it was brought about more out of the need for action than by fear. He always felt that rush amid combat which kept him on his toes. Also, he felt anger. Forever someone had caused trouble for him and his men lately, like Cooper's wife, then the woman yesterday. Now this! Normally, he and the boys struck so fast and sure they got what they wanted and shoved on without a hitch. What was happening to his luck?

Yet gunplay was something men in his profession should expect and always be prepared to face—Zed knew that sure enough, for he'd taken lead more than once in his outlaw career—and presently something other than running was called for. . . .

And with a few swift and curt directions to Bledsoe and the breed, things quickly went to hell for the San Augustine sheriff and his small posse.

Chapter Six

Puffs of gun smoke blossomed on the far side of the open woods. The kid was barreling among the widely spaced pin oaks, shooting wildly. Cooper wondered what was in his mind, charging a defended position single-handedly like that. Then he saw the horse go down and the boy go flying to hit the ground hard. Inevitable with such foolishness!

Volleys were exchanged for several seconds. The kid stirred then and cried out in pain. Spurts of soil erupted about him and he scrambled for shelter behind a tree. "Help me, guys! My leg's busted!"

Lead struck and whined around him with new fervor at that. Tabor was suddenly up and climbing aboard his jittery cayuse, pointing the animal downhill and putting the rowels to it. Cooper concurred with the fellow's logic—no matter how big a fool a man is doesn't mean he should be shot to pieces by vermin like Rodel's bunch—so he also spurred into a gallop. Hunched over the pommel, he rode his black with the purpose of assisting Tabor in the rescue.

Dunigan was, for the most part, hiding his vitals with the huge base of a pine, and he uttered a profanity at the two racing off without having been given an order to do so. Jonas Bretton was feeling fear himself, this being his first gunfight, yet he griped at the sheriff and other man on the wooded terrace with him, "Put yo guns to work! That boy of yours down there will get plugged eventually, and Tabor and Tom need cover fire!"

Jonas flinched at a bullet rattling through the branches of the blackjack he braced the barrel of his rifle against. In short order he laid a string of five .44 balls into the far line of brush and trees and levered a sixth halfway back toward his starting point for good measure. Glad his two companions were finally shooting again and not just looking dazed, he thumbed cartridges into the Winchester's lengthy magazine. While doing so, he heard the pinned-down kid cry out with pain and fear as a hostile shotgun pellet dug into his young flesh.

Tabor reached the crippled boy a few seconds ahead of Cooper and dropped to the ground to help him up on the horse. Tom knew how he could be of most help, and so began levering .56's at the enemy's position, only noises and muzzle flashes in the dense thicket to aim at, if there was even a chance to aim while keeping on the move in a circle. His gelding flinched and side-stepped; Tom realized the animal had been hit, but not how hard, and could do nothing about it anyway. Projectiles sang by him and he fought on until the carbine was empty.

Ungratefully the kid charged for safety the moment his butt met Tabor's saddle, leaving his saviors in the midst of turmoil to fend for themselves with but one horse. Spencer sheathed and Colt drawn, Cooper reined over and offered the abandoned Tabor his left hand and stirrup. The stern gent had lost his hat in the commotion and his bald pate gleamed with sweat. He accepted Tom's help, condemning the brat he had just saved, and, as he swung up behind Tom, the latter thumbed shots in the general direction of their foes, knowing very well the distance was too great for accuracy with the pistol. Heading the mustang after the retreating young man, Cooper hoped the gelding wasn't hurt so bad to prevent him from gaining the ridge with his double burden.

Right before leaving the flat to scramble up the steep incline to the level of the terrace, Tabor grunted and slammed against Cooper's back. Tom reached behind to help support the man, but the position was awkward and Tabor fell. Cooper checked the horse's forward momentum and spun him around. He saw at a glance the cause was lost.

Blood was smeared on the carpet of green bottom grass and dead leaves where Tabor had rolled, and the man's neck lay at an unnatural angle. Tom turned and, with the din of fighting dwindling, urged his mount on up to Jonas's side. He saw that the gelding's wound was only a burn along the flank, was thankful it hadn't been like with the two cavalry mounts he'd lost in the War, then spoke to Jonas while reloading his weapons.

"Mount up and follow me."

Louder rumblings of thunder replaced cracks of gunfire altogether now. Dunigan cursed obscenely. "Where the devil y'all goin'?"

"Try to flank 'em. You three just hold this hill. Think ya can do that right?" Cooper didn't expect an answer and so headed out with Jonas without waiting for one.

It took time to circle cautiously in on Rodel's position, and when they got there all there was to find were metal bullet casings, a few empty shotgun shells, tracks of men and horses, and a few blood stains. Tom hollered all was clear to the others, then, picking up Rodel's dropped rifle, rode with Jonas back to reconnoiter over Tabor's body. He had a hard look and an angry mind while briefly telling that the outlaws had obviously skinned out, still going west and a heck of a lot better off than their own party.

"Well, we drew blood," Dunigan concluded, mounted once again after the third posseman had caught up his escaped horse. "Maybe it'll slow 'em down for the Rangers. We gotta get Tabor and Bart back to town now." He took the Winchester from Cooper.

Bart, the wounded kid, was leaning on the pommel crying, and Tom Cooper eyed him hard. "You know what they did to deserters in the War, boy? Killed 'em, that's what. And the same oughtta be done to you!"

Dunigan wasn't happy with how things had gone or how they were going. "Hey, Cooper, just a durn minute here! Bart made a noble charge!" Actually, the lawman knew the young man's actions for what they were, but he felt he must defend him.

"Stupid's what it was!" Tom fired back. "And when he took the butt of the deal he lost his spine." He frowned at the blubbering Bart and mused he appeared every bit of twelve years old. No, he'd seen boys that age act more of a grown man, and he said so. Then, "He ran out on Tabor down yonder and can be sure he's the reason the man's dead." Cooper pointed down at the corpse. "He was the best man in your sorry outfit, Dunigan, and now he's gone! *For good!*"

Bretton had never known his white friend to be so harsh before the cursed thing which had sent them on this trek, yet, although it was scary, he could understand. Jonas Bretton was caught up in the same whirl-wind, to a degree.

"That's enough!" barked Dunigan, and Tom clenched both hands on the enormous horn of his saddle, designed for the tremendous strain of roping. Dunigan took a deep breath and informed, "Now we got things to see to."

"Darn right we do. You can go on with us while your other man gets the kid and Tabor back to town."

"You ain't runnin' this show, Cooper! *I* am."

Tom sneered. "And a fine job you've done, Sheriff."

Grinding his teeth at the sarcasm, Dunigan stated as calmly as he could, "We're 'bout outta my county. I got to see us back to San Augustine. The Rangers have been sent for."

"But they ain't here!" The air was thick with the energy of tense men and horses and a storm about to break. A streak of lightning ripped across the black sky and struck something very near. Every man and beast jumped save Cooper and his mustang; they just sat firm.

Tom Cooper's voice was hard and blunt as the rumblings in the sky. "Rodel's trail has to be followed while there *is* a trail. It won't last long in a bad rain, and one's a-comin'."

That was true enough, you could smell it, but Dunigan wasn't used to being argued with on orders he gave. "It's not your affair, Cooper, it's the law's. You'll ride back with us, by God."

"Never! You wash your hands of it, that's fine. I won't. Ever."

The sandy-haired man's voice was not loud as he finished, but nonetheless unyielding, and no one opposing him could like his present steely look. The sheriff surely didn't. "And what'll you do if ya catch 'em?" he demanded.

"I reckon that'd be my business."

"Ya got a right to want Rodel and them, Cooper, what with your wife and boy and all. But if I hear you lynched those men, I'll make it *my* business!"

"So be it." And then every man there except Tom breathed easier as he neck-reined west, away from an argument that could become a whole lot uglier than it already was.

"That go for you, too, boy?" Dunigan questioned Jonas as he turned from watching the lean man ride off.

Bretton, in his tornado of thoughts, had not realized he'd paused so long in following Tom. "I reckon ridin' fo' a brand is all right. But I'd rather ride fo' a good *taysha.*"

Sheriff Dunigan cursed and shook his head at the word which meant absolutely nothing to him. He watched Bretton trot away. Stories got around in those days faster by people talking than reading newspapers, and a memory of something he'd once heard came to Dunigan. Someone by the name of Cooper had come out on top of a feud with a Louisiana family some years back over on the Sabine River . . . and this Tom Cooper gent was from over that way.

Rain began to patter down, and Dunigan turned to the task of helping his last able-bodied posseman load Tabor across one of their saddles. It was going to be a slow, tiring trip until they could acquire a replacement for Bart's dead horse at a homestead. After that, Sheriff Dunigan would be finished with this mess. All but telling the Rangers everything he could.

Chapter Seven

Here and there blood-spotted brush and scarred earth helped Tom and Jonas stick to the desperados' trail, but it was tense and miserable going in the weather which threatened to wash out the sign. It was impossible to tell for sure until they came upon the source a mile later if it was a man or horse that had been losing so much blood.

Choctaw Blue's mount lay kicking in the throes of death when they rode up to it. Pulling up, Tom had just gotten his carbine to his shoulder after studying the area for ambushers when it was apparent it was too late to end the animal's suffering. He was dead.

Cooper's shoulders were hunched under the protection of a worn poncho, and the water poured off his brown felt hat to stream down the cloak. He surmised,

"You said ya thought you got into his horse. Now that breed'll be addin' weight to one of the others' nags. Ride ready." And he nudged his mustang on.

Jonas kept his mare slightly back and to the right of Tom, seeing by the way his friend took off that he was anxious. The reason was more than obvious—the rain was increasing in quantity, the storm in strength, and even though one set of the tracks they followed were deeper now, they were becoming harder to see, steadily being obliterated. And no longer were there blood stains to mark the way.

It worried Jonas, too. Would the trail end here?

Crossing through a stand of gums, Tom lost the sign entirely. He leaned over to see the ground better— around noon, the dark heavens made it look more like twilight beneath the heavy timber of the bottom land— and zigzagged to no avail. In yet another wide circle some bruised dogwood saplings and yellow jessamine vines pointed him northwest and soon out onto the Attoyac's eastern bank.

Here there was a low bluff, and no sign of riders anywhere. Everything was slick with wetness and the wind whipped furiously. Odd that it could be so hot a while ago and so chilly now.

Bretton drew alongside Cooper and raised his voice over the noise of the cloudburst. "Tom, let's hole up fo' a break in this weather. We might do more harm than good if we push on blind."

Thunder and lightning disturbed Jonas's sorrel, and even Cooper found himself soothing his gelding when the top was broken out of a nearby willow by a gust of wind. "All right, horses need some rest anyhow."

Yet, as he pulled back in the trees, he didn't like it. Time, time was wasting and ground being lost. . . .

Midafternoon found them back in the saddle and scouring the opposite side of the Attoyac's murky waters. Hitting sign was hopeless and both knew it; mangled vegetation might have just as easily been caused by the summer storm as a passerby. And, while hoofprints were very discernable left by a horse's steps now, a long distance could have been covered by the gang before the rain had stopped. Jonas felt it was Tom's call, though, so he rode in silence, using every bit of his own woodsman's knowledge to aid his comrade.

In doing so, he mulled over what Cooper was going through. Bretton was grieving for Stan and Bell, too, but he knew it was not the same. What if it had been his Ruth?

He hated himself for being thankful it hadn't been. Lord!

Often little Stanly would watch or help him work and ask hundreds of child's questions. Never had Bretton been too busy to take up time with him, however, for he knew that was the way a boy learns and becomes a man. Just a few days before all this, he'd given the boy a team of toy oxen which he'd carved from a piece of cedar.

And Bell, she'd treated him as good as any white hand, something you didn't see much of in the South. By teaching him to read she had bettered his life to a great extent. She and Ruth had gotten along well, and it was supposed to have been a grand life for the black couple when they married. The Coopers would have welcomed her on the place as much as they had Jonas, not just as hired help, but friends—family, really.

Before dark the sun came from behind the clouds and made the thickets feel like ovens. Steam rose from the wet earth and vegetation, and once they crossed a slough off of the Attoyac which held dark water knee deep to the horses. The shallowest of depressions were soggy, and the merest touch would knock showers of huge drops from the trees and brush they perched so precariously on. It was evident tonight wouldn't be one of physical comfort. Mental, neither, for that matter.

Finally Tom turned to him. "Let's stop for the night, Jonas." There was a heavy pause. "What'll I do if I don't pick up their sign?"

Bretton didn't relish at all the desperation in his friend's tone. He put as much confidence as possible in the words. "Jes' keep huntin' and nosin' about till we do. Ain't nothing lives what don't leave clues of its passin'."

* * *

Indeed Rodel and company were quite some way from the bayou by nightfall, in spite of having to ride double. It had been a tough day, but none of them were seriously hurt. Rodel was the worst off with his lacerated gun hand, yet they were all in a black mood because of the circumstances.

"Well, we gotta have another plug 'fore long if the Injun's gonna keep up," Fast Bledsoe speculated to Rodel over a scant supper of hardtack. "He'll kill our horses for sure if we have to push 'em."

"You'd like to leave me behind, wouldn't ya, Bledsoe?" demanded the half-breed with an ugly look from the other side of the campfire.

"Don't get huffy, Blue. I ain't in the mood to kill a saddle partner right now. Not a lone thing's gone right 'cept getting that money off the stage. There was a glitch in even that, losin' Miguel!"

Zed took a swallow of the coffee made from the supply acquired from the Hadzlot farm along with some other grub, the 12 gauge that now was his only long gun, some ammunition for it, and a little over four dollars in silver. "Can't expect everything to go perfect," he soothed. "We'll make out. Always do."

The Choctaw exploded. "I knew it was a bad idea to mess with the women! I tell y'all, I seen Cooper and that hired hand of his in that posse back yonder!"

Zed Rodel cleansed the bullet burn on the back of

his hand, saw that it didn't amount to much save soreness, assured his men they would not be done in by any law or vigilantes, then soon went to bed, uncomfortable in the humid night. Zed intended to live a spell longer; he just wanted to get to his nearest hideout here in Texas, wait a while, then drift and enjoy the cash they had until time for another big job. That wouldn't be so hard if he could just keep his two men away from each other's throat.

His hope of Blue and Bledsoe's bickering coming to a halt for good was ruined, however, with the arrival of the foggy morning.

"All you've done is whine! Where's your backbone, redskin?" Fast Bledsoe scalded Blue with the words when the Choctaw bemoaned his misfortune again, along with the fear he beheld since the killing of Cooper's family.

His eyes orbs of black hate, the Indian grabbed at his knife and started for the young redhead. "I'll show you your own backbone when I cut it out!"

Bledsoe stopped him short by drawing his single-action .44-40 and lining it on his face almost before the Arkansas toothpick cleared the scabbard. The Colt's hammer was at full cock, and, with a sneer on his lightly freckled face, he caressed the trigger. "C'mon, now, Injun, ain't it a good day to die?"

Rodel's scowl contorted further into ugly rage, appearing uncannily evil on his weathered face beneath the shock of white hair. He cursed both his men roundly. "It ain't no time for this! The three of us may be wishin' for the others' guns 'fore it's over! We have to back each other. Now y'all straighten your-selves up!"

Fast Bledsoe kept his gun on Blue's face without wavering as he turned his gaze on the leader. "Aw, Zed, lemme pop 'im. It'll save us some trouble, and me and you can handle things together. He wasn't worth bustin' outta that jail up to Fort Smith. Way he's been acting of late, he'd run out on us if it got bad. Not a good idea to've trusted an Injun, anyway!"

"You wouldn't talk that way if ya didn't have that hogleg, you little skunk," Blue said evenly, letting his deadly blade slip back into its sheath.

Rodel rose from where he squatted, holding the 12 gauge at waist level in the general direction of both men. "You two better dry up and remember who's running this outfit!"

Fast Bledsoe chose to let it ride, because no matter how much he'd given thought to calling Zed Rodel out, he knew the man had no honor. While Bledsoe got a thrill from beating a man in an even break, Rodel was the sort to slink off from a duel and strike after the challenger turned his back. So he didn't consider himself showing the white feather upon holstering the Colt and allowing that Zed *did* call the shots.

Rodel inhaled slowly, letting it out even slower as

he lowered the twin muzzles of the greener. His own moral nature made him distrustful to turn away from Bledsoe. The kid spooked him, and to overcome it Rodel had to rule with an iron hand, yet still make the kid believe he was his number one. In reality, however, Zed's was a dog-eat-dog band, and they all knew it. If you were not needed or wanted, you could be done away with at leisure.

"We're gonna go on pert' near as before, once we get Blue a mount," vowed Rodel. "Fast can go on into Malloy and get provisions when we get close, then drift on to the hideout to meet us." He'd feel much better riding alone to his hole with the Choctaw than with the kid.

Fast Bledsoe caused Zed to halt halfway to his chestnut by saying, "I think I'm gonna drift my own way after hoorawin' some in Malloy. Nothin' personal, just want a try at frying my own fish."

"You'll bring Blue and me some grub and ammunition, *first*," the bandit stated.

The young man conceded with a shrug, going to his horse, but mused he'd do like he pleased once away from Rodel. A man needed to look out for his own interest; they had long since divvied up the loot amongst them, Miguel's share included. *It's high time Fast Bledsoe has his own gang,* he thought. He was tired of taking orders.

"What's the plan about gettin' me a horse, Zed?" Blue questioned while waiting for them to saddle up.

"Have to find somebody that's got some on hand." Rodel swung up and indicated Blue could double with him first this morning. "I'll lay us out an idee whenever an opportunity arises.

"Now let's get. Daylight's a-burnin'."

The following day found Cooper and Bretton further west but still riding blind. The solid-black gelding looked not so shiny after many miles of riding through dirt and water. However, it was a stayer and had plenty of bottom. Despite being the oldest, it was the best mount on the Circle C. The mustang, even now in the sultry heat of midmorning, went at a pace that could wear down many a taller animal, and Tom sent him winding through chaparral and across wooded hills with great intent, hoping today wouldn't be like the futile one they'd spent searching after the gunfight.

Jonas's blond sorrel was quite ready for a rest by the time Cooper called for one. Her flaxen mane and tail were stained with sweat and mud, entangled with leaves and other debris, and Jonas set about cleaning it up by using his fingers as a comb. His hands needed something to do while his mind worked.

He didn't like the quietness that was between them, yet he knew not what to say to his friend whose life had been so devastated, and hoped just his presence offered some support. Tom would talk after he came to terms with things, if he could.

Presently the strong-built man hunkered in the shade of a magnolia, wiped the sweatband of his dirty, wide-brimmed hat, then set it down low on his head to hide his haggard eyes while building a cigarette. He sat there hunched forward while smoking, a deep turmoil in him that could only be fully understood by someone who had lost a loved one to human violence. All the trouble he'd seen during his life didn't seem fair to him in the least. How his mind did spin!

He stubbed out the butt and went to his horse, patting its neck, not wishing to use the animal up, yet needing to make haste at the same time. A horsefly bit him and he slapped at it and swore harder than was the usual for him, with such ardor in fact that the gelding rolled his eyes and fidgeted. Tom hawked, spat, and directed Jonas, "Swing a little wider of me but keep in hearing distance. All we can do is drift west. See somethin', give a holler." The tone of his voice told Jonas well enough what Tom was fighting inside.

Bretton also felt an anxiety upon stepping into the leather. He reined off about a hundred yards to zigzag parallel to his friend's course. They had crossed a wagon trace right after dawn, but at the point of their juncture only a single set of hoofprints marked a passing since the storm. And those tracks showed to be of a horse pulling a buggy. Absolutely no sign of a horseback trio. No riders at all!

Had they lost the trail for good? This evening would make some forty-eight hours without a single bit of sign.

Drinking from his canteen, Bretton scanned the wooded terrain as he jammed the stopper back down and frowned at the taste of the tepid water. It couldn't just dead-end like this! Noon would be here soon, bringing with it more heat and less hope.

A couple of fields of cotton and corn were passed, signifying there were some occupants inhabiting this hinterland forest. But all seemed peaceful, and they trotted on without trying to locate the owners of the growing crops. Truly this was sparsely populated country.

Beyond a grassy savannah of several acres in size they entered a big stand of shortleaf pines, the ground beneath them covered with brown needles and littered with dead limbs and small cones. Also evident was where squirrels had fed on the burs here and there; even now Jonas saw a big one break from its secluded rest on a high bough. The reddish-orange rodent traveled the timber out of the man's vision, barking coarsely in its throat.

Cooper, at the same time, was oblivious of nature's goings-on. He rode alert in the saddle, though. Alert for what he sought—the killers of his family.

Abruptly he drew up and listened. "Jonas!" he called. "Come here!"

Bretton guided his sorrel up beside him within moments, a look of anticipation on his dark face. "Hear that?" Cooper asked him.

"Somebody's sawin'."

Cooper nodded. "Sounds like a whole passel of loggers. Let's see if they've seen anything strange. I got a bad feelin' I should've done so at them farms back yonder." He turned south along a little draw.

The drain emptied into a shallow piney-woods branch and Tom followed its trickling course toward the noise of the saws. Bretton trooped along in the rear, sending up a quiet prayer that something would turn up. Anything helpful. It was all too likely Rodel and his men had altered their plan of heading for the hideout the Mexican had said was near the Neches, and swung in a different direction since they knew they were being hounded.

That worried Jonas, for the older a trail got the harder it was to track; that was common sense. And he and Tom, they had clearly lost the way.

Up a long, gradual rise after passing through an area where resin-wet stumps and sheared limbs—their needles still green—marked a fresh cutting, the pair came to where about a dozen men were busy with crosscut saws and double-bit axes. Tom walked his black up to a couple of fellows working the sharp teeth of one of the former tools into the thick trunk of a loblolly, and they stopped to straighten their backs and stare at him. Tom queried about the outfit's boss.

The skinny one with missing front teeth jerked a thumb up the hill. "The guy up there by the slip-tongue. The big one in the overalls."

Cooper spurred on, leaving the flatheads to their job of felling trees. The husky gent in the overalls was working with another man to hook three heavy logs up to the slip-tongue cart with a four-up mule team right past some limbers busy with their axes, trimming more downed trees.

Introducing himself, Tom declined the offer from the head of the logging operation to step down, then related his plight in brief. The burly logging boss gave his sympathy.

"It so happens I can help ya," he added, hand on one of the two nine-foot cart wheels. "An Indian fella walked into our camp right early this mornin' after breakfast. Thought it strange, him being alone and afoot so far from nowhere—we been cuttin' here nigh on to a week and ain't seen a soul 'cept while hauling the logs to the river, and that's a right far piece—but ya see all kinds passin' through these days.

"Anyhow, if I'd known he's connected with that outlaw Rodel, I'd have had nothin' to do with 'im."

Tom Cooper's impatience showed. "I ain't blaming you, man. Just tell me what he did, where he went!"

"Well, he wanted a mount and offered good money. All I could afford to be shed of was a crazy bay mule that wasn't makin' good work stock. I . . . I sold 'im. Got forty dollars and the guy rode off bareback. He went down our loggin' road yonder towards the river."

Elation surging in him like it was Tom, Bretton gave their appreciation and started after Cooper who just waved his hand in farewell. The ruts and drag marks, gouged in the soil by the heavy vehicles and ends of the pulled logs respectively, wound slowly down to lower ground. Riders and horses sweated, especially when traversing the narrow lanes the loggers had hacked through jungle-like thickets to get the felled trees to the Angelina River. Not much could be discerned from the multitudes of scars in the wet ground, but they rode on with more hope than before. Twice they passed empty carts with their drivers heading back for the next load astride the nearside wheeler, answering to the negative had they seen any strangers on the trail. Tom and Jonas finally came to the stream bed after several miles of steady riding in the grueling heat.

A clearing was situated here atop a steep bank and was marked by the turning around of many slip-tongues and their teams. A logjam filled the swollen river from bank to bank, the great number of logs fastened together by another crew of men into rafts to be sent downstream to a sawmill further south. Indeed it could sometimes be a long process to get the trees from where they were harvested to a place they could be turned into lumber. It was hard but honest work.

At being quizzed, the head man of this part of the job told Bretton and Cooper, "No, ain't saw nobody today but our boys. There's a ferry upstream a good ways that'll make the ford easier for you, bein' as the water's up." He thanked them for the warning about Rodel in the area as they pushed on in the late afternoon.

Bretton took a chance an hour later to intrude on Tom's solitude. "You'se think that Injun broke off from 'em on his own? Mebbe they left 'im behind like they done the Mex."

Tom was studying the loamy earth at the edge of a wide distributary they were about to cross. He looked out across the bayou stretching darkly among water-loving trees where it spilled out of the river. This slough befitted the term swamp, and Cooper pointed down at the muck along its edge to what had held his attention.

"No. They're together. And, by God, we're on their trail." As they had been for the last few days, Cooper's words were hard and clipped. A sharp intensity was about his whole being.

Bretton's eyes went to what he indicated in the twilight. In the mud on a space void of anything to hinder their prints were the tracks of a small group of horses, one of which had the notable chip missing from its shoe.

Chapter Eight

It was the season for serpents to be about, so they made camp there, back a little way from the swamp, planning to cross the flooded stretch come good daylight. A dank smell permeated the air in the Angelina Bottom—the extreme wetness of these places was the very reason why most settlers built their homes and fields on terraces out of the low areas, just near enough for their cows and hogs to be able to forage down into them—and Tom did not like the feel of his body and clothing, sticky with grime in the warm twilight. He saw to the weary horses, then washed very little jerky and stale biscuits down with the coffee Bretton had made, only grunting at Jonas's comment that they would need more staples soon.

Jonas poured himself another cup from the blackened pot and leaned against his saddle. He'd not pressure his distraught friend for conversation, thus silence prevailed. By the waning light of the fire Tom began to clean and oil his weapons, and Jonas sipped his coffee and watched a few minutes before tending to his Winchester that had also been out in the elements.

Tom started with his Colt Army, its blued steel and walnut grip shining ominously in the circle of firelight. From talk Jonas knew of Tom's past as a fighting man, yet Jonas had never seen him in a battle until that one on the ridge. In the time he'd known Cooper, the most amazing thing he had seen from the man in the form of gun handling was putting one of the big Spencer slugs straight into a hog's ear at over sixty yards across an open stretch of Sabine River bottom.

One could not doubt from the attention Tom gave his guns now that he knew about using them for more than just stock and game. After checking the smoothness of the cleaned .44's single action, he thumbed bright cartridges into all six chambers of the cylinder. He coated the inside of the holster with just a touch of oil before returning the weapon to the leather and beginning work on his carbine.

While dumping the loads from the tubular magazine located in the Spencer's butt, and ejecting the one in the chamber, Tom thought of the men he'd used his guns on. Never had he hunted trouble; it always just came to *him.* He bitterly concluded that it was his lot in life as he rubbed the cloth reverently over stock, breech, forearm, and barrel. He'd been taught the care of firearms by his pa and the Union Army, had seen its usefulness firsthand. A gun, like a horse, could not be depended on if it wasn't seen after.

Reloading the long gun, he thought severely, *Because of Rodel and his men, I'll not get to see my son grow up with those or any other lessons.*

He caught a glimpse of Jonas watching him upon jacking a fresh load into the Spencer's chamber. Bretton cleared his throat, looked away, then back, and asked, "You think we'll catch up soon?"

"I hope. Wantta be ready when*ever* we do."

Quiet then, just the croaking of frogs and swarming of mosquitoes along the swamp. Jonas Bretton's dark eyes were deep and luminous in the flickering light, and Cooper felt those eyes still on him as he put away the cleaning supplies and laid the guns in easy reach. He dwelled on Jonas and their relationship, leaning forward to drain the last of the coffee from the pot. One swallow told him there were too many grounds for his taste, and he slung the mess from his cup. His thoughts were yet heavy about Bretton when the latter returned from a trip to relieve himself in the shadows.

Cooper started fashioning a smoke and began, "I got no right draggin' you into this, Jonas. It's my affair to see after, not yours. The place'll need somebody who knows it lookin' after it, and I'd be obliged if you'd head back there and do just that."

"I reckon you may need more help than the farm. You'se taken a tough job in hand, and I wantta help ya see it through. If the law ain't 'bout to do it, it makes sense somebody else's got to do it."

Tom offered him the makings and Jonas accepted the sack of Durham and book of rolling papers. Jonas wasn't as adept in the art of building a cigarette because he was not a habitual smoker, but like now, in idle moments, he indulged. So he slowly got one made, though it was crude, and inhaled it to life as they sat in silence.

Cooper said abruptly, "I don't mean to be so short lately. For the kinda friend you've been, I been a buzzard to ya. . . . There's no excusin' it, it's just—"

"We'se been through all that befo'," the other cut in. "If there be any man who's got a right to be sore at the world, it's one that's been through what you have." At the same time, Bretton silently hoped once the killers were brought to justice, one way or another, that Tom could put the bitterness behind him and go on with his life.

"Sure ya won't head back? I'd think nonetheless of ya."

Jonas Bretton shook his burly head. "I never went against another man with nothin' mo' than my fists.

But I guess I can hold that rifle of mine steady enough to stand beside ya."

Tom was sure of that, himself. While Jonas didn't look for or like trouble, either, he was not the type to crawfish when it raised its head. He'd seen the Jonas belly up and take control of some mighty rank livestock. In fact, Jonas was the best hand Tom had seen at looping a hog with a throw rope. The man was reliable in a tight.

"Feel better with somebody watchin' my back." Cooper took a last drag, thumped the butt into the dying fire, and declared, smoke exiting with the words, "We'll cross this slough soon as we can see good. Oughtta get to that ferry pretty soon."

Jonas felt more at ease after their bit of talk, and he soon bedded down. As he stretched out atop his blankets, the long, deep bellow of an alligator sounded from somewhere out in the dark bottom which was its home. The noise was foreboding to Cooper, and a chill ran the length of his spine.

"Hope the light don't bother you, but I'm hopin' the smoke will keep the mosquitoes at bay," he remarked, tossing more fuel on the red coals.

Pulling his hat over his eyes, Bretton gave a half-hearted chuckle. "I tolerate it in hopes it'll keep away bigger varmints that bite. I knew of a fella what got dragged off in his sleep by a 'gator on a sandbar down on the Brazos."

Tom allowed how anything is possible and scrunched down against his saddle. Of a sudden there was a bad feeling in him, like a dark premonition concerning his fate. However, it had nothing to do with any cold-blooded creatures that sported more than two legs.

Always Tom Cooper had been one to give thought to the future. And now he used the growing flames of the fire for yet another purpose. By the firelight he took the business papers from the inside pocket of his vest and, using a stub of pencil, wrote on the envelope which held them.

He could tell from his slow, even breathing that Jonas had already drifted off, and he was glad for the privacy to do this. The documents back in his vest, Cooper lay back but couldn't relax.

It was ironic that he and Bell, brought together so fast under harsh and violent circumstances, had then been torn apart even faster by some of the same. Tears filled his eyes at thinking of times he'd been short with her and Stanly. Though he knew such things were normal in all families, it hurt him. And he regretted every single time. Wiping his eyes and bearded cheeks, he switched his thoughts forcefully from his sadness to the hate for the men who caused it. And what he would do about it.

The night wore on without sleep, and he suddenly had a strong feeling he'd be with his wife and child again very soon. It was an odd, prophetic thought which wouldn't go away, yet it was not altogether unsettling to him. He only prayed he could punish Zed Rodel and the other two men—first. Then, he'd just as soon be with his wife and son than in this cursed world.

Tom's senses became alert to something suddenly. Unlike earlier, there were no night sounds now, and it made him uneasy. Especially with his ominous feeling.

With the Spencer he arose after several minutes of careful listening, checked the horses, and walked stealthily around the campsite to be sure no one was about. He returned to his blankets not much better off. The loss of his wife and child was a terrible void within him, and he could not say he was eager to live on this earth beyond the time of seeing Rodel's gang get what they deserved. So what if something happened to him then, as long as he got those heathens?

He would see after his loyal comrade's future, though. His hand went to the slight bulge of papers in his vest, and it was those documents and what he had written that was still on his mind when he finally slept.

Chapter Nine

Somewhere high up in the timber a locust buzzed as the two men trotted their horses up the east bank of the Angelina River in the midmorning heat. No more tracks had they found upon crossing the slough they had camped on, bringing a curse from Tom after a thorough, time-consuming search—he hoped the killers hadn't doubled back—and so he and Jonas were now pushing on to the ferry. They reached it within a quarter-hour.

Tom looked down from his seat on the mustang at the damp ground on the riverbank where the flat craft was moored to a leaning cypress. "Yeah! They've been here. See that chipped shoe print?"

Affirming that he did, Bretton led the way over a small opening on their right to the operator's quarters just off a rutted track coming to the waterway from the northeast. The gray shack was square, tiny, had no porch, and was made of undressed cypress lumber. A thin curl of smoke came out of a rusty pipe protruding from the much-mended roof.

It was an ancient but spry gent in baggy overalls with a patch over his left eye and a bandage around his head who greeted them sternly from just inside the narrow doorway, the latter shaded by a bushy chinaberry tree which grew right against the house. "Yeah, what?"

"We need use of your ferry," explained Cooper.

The old man came out on the steps, and only then could it be seen he carried a big percussion buffalo gun in one hand. "Be four bits apiece." His one eye squinted as he took in their appearance warily.

"Whatever you say, Mister. But let's get at it. We're in a hurry!" Tom was more than impatient.

"Young folk's *always* in a hurry," he muttered, walking out to the heads of their horses and peering up at the riders' faces. Still he kept a secure grip on the big muzzleloader. "Y'all some kinda law?"

Cooper took a deep breath. He'd been taught to respect elders, and this man reminded him a lot of his dead father-in-law. "No, sir. But we *are* after some outlaws."

"I figure I seen those you're talkin' 'bout." He squirted tobacco juice with a sideways jerk of his head and shifted the quid in a toothless mouth. "What they wanted for besides robbin' me?"

"They robbed ya?" Bretton queried.

The old-timer dipped his chin, and Tom surmised, "You can claim yourself lucky for bein' able to walk." Then he poured out who they were after and what their latest crimes were.

The ferryman swore at the criminals' brutality before speculating, "If I'd laid eyes on 'em, they would've likely sent me to the next world, too." He pointed a rough thumb at the strip of white cloth around his head. "Was laid out cold by some varmint when I come outside to investigate a racket yesterday afternoon. Never knew nothin' till it was all over and done. They found my cash box and cleaned it out. I had to use my dugout to go over and get the ferry from where they left it on the other side, dang 'em!"

"Right sorry about that. You can see why they gotta be dealt with." Tom was ready to be moving.

"Sure thing," the grizzled fellow asserted. "But first how 'bout a good feed for you boys and your plugs? Blast if it don't look like y'all need it! No offense."

"I thank ya kindly for the offer," Tom started to refuse, "but we—"

"Son, I've rode many a long trail, and I can tell ya thirty minutes ain't gonna ruin your chances by a whole helluva lot. Them coyotes have more'n twelve hours on y'all.

"Now I got corn for your mounts and grub for you two. I was just fixin' myself a late breakfast, and there's plenty of it if'n ya ain't choosy 'bout your vittles."

Tom hesitated and Jonas reasoned, "We ate jerky and biscuits for two days, Tom. And the stock's had nothin' but grass and switch cane and such browse. We'd all do a lot better on the trail with full bellies."

There was logic in the other two's talk and Tom knew it. All the stiffness in the old man had been replaced with an amiable desire to be helpful. Perhaps some conversation with him over a meal would turn up something else useful, such as where exactly the town of Malloy was.

When Tom finally voiced submittal the ferryman headed for the shack at a lively pace, telling them he'd have the fare dished up by the time they fed their horses around back at a lot and shed that was completely vacant of any occupant. The pair removed the bridles and dumped a healthy quantity of the large yellow grain in the lone trough, yet they left the saddles on, just loosened the girths. Striding for the little house, Tom commented to his companion he meant to pay for this hospitality. Jonas fully agreed.

Daylight came into the single-room house via gaps between the upright boards which were its walls as much as did through the open door and windows. Not one unnecessary item took up space in the old-timer's hovel, and the biggest pieces of furniture were the plain bunk built into a corner and the pot-bellied stove on the opposite side. Casually, Cooper and Bretton were told they could wash up, if they so wished, at a chipped pan on a shelf just inside the front door.

"Don't make me no never mind," assured the ferry-man. "Ain't no formality called for at this here place."

Both men did so, and, drying his hands on a piece of feed sack that hung by a nail, Bretton glanced up to the rafters to see a black widow spider sitting comfortably on her web. A shiver touched Jonas's back; he'd stand his ground to the worst livestock there was, but spiders gave him the jitters. A granddaddy had run up his pants' leg once, and he'd danced a jig until he got out of the presence of some ladies so he could disrobe.

"By the way, name's Laz Chadabough," their host told them while motioning to cedar-branch chairs at the small plank table. He took a seat on a large crate.

"I'm Tom Cooper and this is Jonas Bretton. We're much obliged to ya."

Tom winced upon tasting the coffee, and not because of its temperature. The black liquid was close to being equivalent to the consistency of the Angelina's mud out front. And strong—Lord, it was stout! The sourdough bread had obviously been made on a day other than this one, but the best part of the "breakfast" were the pinto beans. They were fine, seasoned well with sow-belly and jalapeños, so the two guests set to, using as little drink as possible to rinse down the food.

The eating was serious yet there was a mite of talk, Chadabough's part issuing from rubbery lips that contorted continuously as he gummed the food. He was sure sorry for Tom's loss—they discussed the notoriety of Zed Rodel—and Cooper quickly came to like the old ferryman. None of the conversation was lighthearted, but low and serious as Bretton helped his friend give a more detailed account of the past days.

Chadabough put a hand gently to his skull and mused, "Last time I was plagued with such headaches was right after that Mex army officer got my eye with the wallop from his musket down in Chihuahua. Knocked it clean out, it did. . . .

"But with a devil like Rodel, indeed I'm lucky. They didn't even take my gun. Then again, not many put much store in cap-locks anymore."

He gave a tenor chuckle. "If'n I'd got the chance I'd have showed at least one of 'em what a .68 caliber ball does to a feller's innards." His voice hardened. "Lots of badmen runnin' 'round the country these days, but it takes a particular kind of evil to hurt women and kids. Most of your common owl hoots and man killers won't do it at all. . . .

"But Rodel's gang . . . well, they gotta be done away with. And I wish you boys luck, I sure do."

Jonas noticed the severity in Tom as they both accepted second helpings of bread and beans. The black man wondered himself how things would turn out. A resolve had settled over him, however, since arguing with Cooper about what to do with the Mexican, and he told himself he was ready—to face violence with violence.

"Think you'll be all right?" Tom questioned after some quiet, save the sounds of bolting a meal, pointing to Chadabough's bandaged head.

"Aw, yeah! I may be old as Methuselah, but I'm still a bull of the woods. Come way back from fightin' stock, I do; great-grandpap fought under Washington to get independence from smart-aleck England, and Papa and an older brother of mine died in the War of 1812. And me, I could tell ya some hair-raisin' stories!

"A feller either goes under or learns how to overcome a lot when he's been knocked around as much as myself—survivin' the Mexican War, pannin' gold in Californy with the other forty-niners, then workin' my way over hard country and through scalp-huntin' Injuns back to Texas. Huh, why I figure I've lived more good years than a cutthroat like Rodel ever will! A man that's got meanness in 'im don't ever come to no good.

"My nephew'll be in with supplies tomorrow. He

comes once a week. I'll get 'im to notify the law in these parts, maybe they'll be more help than them others you spoke of. At least hurry the Rangers up. Trash like Rodel's bunch has gotta be dealt with."

Cooper pushed the last bite onto his fork with a piece of sourdough. "What do ya know about a town called Malloy, somewhere on toward the Neches?"

"Not much that's good, and that's a fact. Why?"

Jonas was at ease with this elderly white man, and he answered, "We'se got reason to believe one or more of Rodel's bunch'll be ridin' in there, and it'd help us to knows how to get there."

"That's easy enough to tell," presumed Chadabough, finishing the meal with a long draught of his bitter brew. "Hit the road on the other side of the river yonder and stay with it till it forks. Take the one that angles southwest, and it'll run right through the town."

Cooper stood, ignoring the want of a smoke because time couldn't be taken for such right then, and Jonas excused himself with the statement he'd fetch the horses. Tom suffered a token sip of his hardly touched coffee, suppressed a grimace, and asked Chadabough what he had meant with the slur about the town before they followed Bretton out.

The man stopped and turned his single eye squarely on Tom. " 'Cause it's a roughneck sawmill town where violence is commonplace. Sure, there's bound to be a few decent folks in the vicinity, but they sure ain't the majority. Those that ain't shifty locals, are mean transients. The folks thereabouts look out for themselves.

"It's just the sorta place that'd cater to the likes of those that run with Rodel. And there's plenty others of milder caliber who'd still stick a blade in your ribs for the price of a bottle of the cheap whiskey they serve there. So you and your man be careful, son. It ain't a good place."

Nodding his understanding, Cooper walked out with him, took the reins of his horse Jonas brought around with his own, and followed Chadabough's pert step down the gentle grade to the river. The ferryman was indeed lively for his age, every bit a match for the Angelina's current which bobbled his craft. He refused all offers of help from his two clients in crossing the swollen waterway, and propelled the narrow, railed barge along its taut guide ropes with a long pole, while Cooper and Bretton stood with their mounts watching the murky stream. Disembarking the tied-up ferry on the western shore, both men produced dollar bills from the pockets of their jeans with the intent of paying for the old-timer's hospitality.

Chadabough had his toothless mouth busy situating a generous wad of tobacco from a deer-hide pouch, so he shook his head vigorously, grunting "Uh-uh" until he was able to speak. "I didn't do all I done for money. You boys just get them sons of Satan!"

Extending his greenback further, Bretton surmised respectfully, "We're sho obliged, Mister Chadabough, and want to pay ya. Mebbe it helps a little since you'se been robbed."

The old-timer waved his gnarled hands and protested, "Thanks, but I got a mite stashed back where nobody'd find it. They didn't take from me near what they did from y'all. If Rodel and his hooligans is done away with, all mankind will be far to the good."

There was no use in arguing with the sincere old gentleman, and the pair realized it. So, withdrawing the money and swinging up, they headed off on the road after again voicing true gratitude.

Over a mile fell behind the horses' rumps as the men traveled in a humid, summer silence, the kind of noisy silence only known on a ride through heavy woodlands, before Cooper spoke up to tell his companion Chadabough's warning about Malloy.

Jonas pushed back his stained hat with a thumb and reflected, "There ain't a human that lives what don't have some faults, and I reckon Laz Chadabough's got his." He laughed for the first time since this had all begun. "Lord knows his coffee'll take the hair off a boar hog! But he sho struck me as a good-ol' cuss."

"World would be a sight better with more of his kind and less of those like the ones we're after." Cooper wondered if he could ever get shed of the fury which swelled in him at the mere thought of Rodel and his gang.

Chapter Ten

Zed and his men kept away from the main road whenever it passed near human habitations, yet they made good time on it when the coast was clear. The weather was fine, just hot as Hades, and there had been no trouble for them since the confrontation east of the Attoyac. So Rodel felt more at ease. He talked confidently, turned an occasional glance to their back trail, but for the most part he kept his eyes and attention on what lay ahead. It never did much good to worry over the past, anyway.

Bledsoe was eager for a blowout in Malloy, couldn't wait to be on his own. Once he enjoyed some of his stake he'd be off to start his own operation, pick and rule his own men. Zed wasn't enough of a chance-taker to suit Bledsoe. Like with playing cards or any such gambling, you had to be bold and face risks if you were going to make it big as an outlaw.

It was true enough Rodel had made notoriety. But not like that which Fast Bledsoe planned for himself. Instead of hit-and-run guerilla raids like those of so many gangs during and since the War, Bledsoe wanted the acclaim of being a greatly feared gunman.

The young man grinned at Rodel's back while trotting along and thought, *Then again, old Zed hasn't ever been the gun hand I am.*

Bledsoe could throw a six-shooter as well as any man he'd seen, better than all those he'd drawn against. Thus he walked with a swagger, the Colt low and ready on his hip. And he'd been around a good deal despite his few number of years. Already people knew his name in Alexandria, Baton Rouge, Fort Smith, Tahlequah, and various little places in between.

Now he figured it was time to work his way further west. Say the Big Bend Country, then maybe El Paso and on out to Santa Fe. He'd be a bandit leader who'd match guns with anybody who thought they were good enough. He had the recklessness of youth which made one sneer at death.

Choctaw Blue jounced along with them, irked at the mount he was forced to ride. The bay jack mule he'd bought from the timberman stood no less than sixteen hands and would push fourteen hundred pounds, but he was not reliable in the least. First off, it was painful to ride without a saddle—the mule wasn't fond of a man on his back, showed it every chance he got—and the only headgear that had been provided with the animal was a worn hackamore. Too, because he'd been broke for work stock and not riding, he was not schooled in the technique of neck-reining. Added to this was the fact the beast shied and acted up at the slightest provocation. He was a perpetual bugger hunter, big eyes and long ears constantly in search of something to bolt from. And his gait, it would beat the kidneys out of a man if you put him into what was for him a canter.

Blast, why couldn't that old codger of a ferryman have had a nag I could steal? Blue thought with irritation.

Zed drew up at a fork in the road. "Now me and Blue are gonna stop shy of the hideout by a couple miles, Fast. Just so we're sure about the back trail 'fore goin' in, ya know.

"You don't dilly-dally in town too long. We'll be needin' supplies. Besides the usual, I want some double-aught buckshot for this greener. This squirrel-shot that sodbuster had for it don't tear near big enough holes to suit me."

Bledsoe gave the merest of nods before spurring south. A glance over his shoulder told him the other two were on their way in the opposite direction, and he fully intended it to be the last time he'd lay eyes on them.

Allowing Blue to come alongside him on the road northwest, Rodel confided, "I'm gettin' tired of that smug little pup. I think purty soon me and you would be better off without 'im."

The Choctaw drew his long, double-edged knife with a malicious grin, and sunlight glinted on the fine steel. "You give me notice ahead of time, and he'll never make a sound."

Steadily Cooper and Bretton ascended into sandy uplands from the Angelina River valley. Chunks of sandstone lined and dotted the road, so tracks, save a few wagon ruts, became increasingly harder to discern. They made good time before dark. The men spent the night after crossing the river just off the highway in a grove of sumac and ironwood on the bank of a little stream fed by spring water cascading over slabs of soapstone, and in the morning they pushed on along the thoroughfare into giant stands of virgin longleaf pine, totally barren of underbrush for great distances in the rolling hills. Early, the air was quite comfortable, and speed could be gained. Around midmorning they came to the crossroads Chadabough had spoken of the day prior.

"Where's to? It's yo call." Bretton quirted his mount's strong neck with the reins, aggravated at her griping at his directions. She'd nipped at him this morning upon being bridled and had been spunky ever since. Jonas knew it was only because she had come in, yet you still had to show a horse who's boss.

Tom had talked it all over with his friend the evening before—they had weighed the pros and cons of what direction to take when getting here, but had decided nothing for sure. Now he shrugged. "They haven't deviated from what that Mex said so far, so I bet Bledsoe is in Malloy. I want *him* as well as the other two. Reckon that means we're headin' into that rough little burg."

Jonas wiped his face and surmised, "Let's go. I been to rough places befo'."

He checked his mare's progress after covering some hundred yards and pointed to a spot of damp white sand. "You're right."

Tom saw he indicated a print of the chipped horseshoe which they hadn't seen in a while, all morning in fact. "Must belong to Bledsoe's plug. C'mon," he said, spurring his mustang into quick motion, "that track was made sometime late yesterday."

Within the next five miles the road to the south by a little west got much narrower. It went through tracts of newly cut timber, and acres of secondary growth with slim pine saplings towering over thickets of hardwoods, vine-tangled brush, and palmetto. A nice buck with velvet on his antlers cleared the path ahead of them in a single bound, and just as they came into faint hearing of the whining, steam-powered sawmill, homes began to appear. However, they were few in number until the men topped a rise and trotted into what passed for a street.

Bretton shucked his Winchester from the boot in front of his right leg, and Cooper removed the thong from the hammer of his Colt. Both men's gazes never halted long on one thing, but continued to scan from beneath the broad, lowered brims of their hats.

A motley assortment of abodes was scattered about the edges of the village—houses of finished lumber, log cabins, clapboard and stone shanties, plumb down to ragged canvas tents. A young boy was out in a small barbed-wire lot, rigging a straight-backed plow horse with a piece of saddle. Just over and down the way was a haggard-looking woman hoeing around some pepper and tomato plants inside a picket fence.

Closer into the town proper, Tom glimpsed a summer-gaunt, black-and-white hog rooting around the backside of a toilet, and he grimaced at seeing another youngster in bare feet playing with a little spotted feist in the filth of an alley. Rubbish was also strewn about the street on ahead between the two rows of buildings. At this hour just prior to noon, the town of Malloy was a quiet place, save for the racket at the south end where the mill was situated which gave the town reason for being here.

Nevertheless, Tom Cooper couldn't say he liked what he saw. No evidence of a church or school—yet there were two saloons. And one of them advertised a cathouse on the second story.

The first business they came to was a blacksmith shop and livery stable of shoddy appearance, and without a word the pair stepped down. A husky black man cut his eyes at them from where he was shaping a piece of iron at the forge. Bretton, with his rifle, and Tom, with his hand on the butt of his revolver, strode through the large entrance very alert.

"What can I do fo' ya?" the smith questioned, straightening to his full height, sledgehammer dangling in a beefy hand by a powerful arm.

"Looking for a man named Bledsoe, called Fast Bledsoe," Cooper said evenly.

"Don't know 'im." The big man went right back to hammering with fervor.

Cooper raised his voice above the metallic ringing. "What about *seen* him? Young, red hair, they say he's chain lightning with a six-shooter."

The bear of a man, naked from the waist up, gleamed with sweat and just shook his head. Jonas could see Tom was losing patience, could hear it in the words: "Do you own this place?"

A flick of his big wrist sent the tongs and piece of iron hissing into a bucket of water. "Yeah! You got a problem with a black man ownin' a business?"

In one long step Jonas Bretton used his rifle barrel to knock the sledge out of the fellow's paw, then backed him against the wall by the anvil with the weapon's muzzle hard on his windpipe. "What he's got a problem with is yo attitude. Bledsoe rides with some men what killed his wife and boy, and they's friends of mine, just like he is. . . . Got it?"

All the belligerence left the smith, and the whites of his eyes were evident as he nodded weakly with the gun cocked and against his throat. He drew a hacking breath as Bretton let up some and growled, "Now I'm as black as you, so there won't be no carpetbagger law sniffin' around if I were to bend yo skull a mite! And that's sho what I'm gonna do if ya don't get real polite and give straight answers."

"I swear, man, I don't know nothin'! Now either kill me or get outta my shop." He was breathing hard but making no threatening moves.

Tom called from where he had strode further back into the building, "Ease up, Jonas. Let's go."

Giving it some consideration, Bretton did. He joined Cooper and headed back for their horses. Mounted, he walked his mare down the street beside Tom and the gelding. They were out of earshot of the livery when the latter man spoke.

"He was lyin'. I saw that chipped shoe print in the dust of the barn's runway. Wasn't no use pressing him, but thanks. We'll just nose Bledsoe out ourselves, but walk soft while we do it."

Jonas nodded and climbed down with him in front of the first saloon. The horses tied to the hitch rail, they mounted a battered sidewalk and crossed to the threshold. Just inside the batwing doors both took in the few occupants prior to striding up to the bar. A dumpy man with the looks of a drunk met them, staring hard with reddened eyes at Bretton.

"Whiskey," ordered Tom, knowing he might get more assistance if he purchased a drink.

Bretton laid his Winchester on the rough, liquor-stained counter and said, "I'll take a beer."

"You'll get nothin' here but my boot in your back if ya don't get out. I don't serve your kind in my place." The words were low and even, directed at Jonas.

It was Cooper who lost his temper this time. In a flash he reached forward and pulled the barkeep over the counter to peer directly into his bloodshot eyes. "He's with me, and he'll drink with me. Understand?"

Bretton soothed Cooper, "Don't worry 'bout it, Tom. I'll mosey on 'cross the street."

Ever so slowly, Tom released the man to pour his drink as Jonas picked up his gun and departed. Cooper realized the last thing he and Jonas needed was to be run out of town. True, there was no law in this hole in the road, but the general populace could do it. So he sipped his drink and tried to quell his angry nerves before asking about the villain they sought. Their quizzing in itself could well draw enough attention to them.

The establishment across the street was of a slightly higher class than the other, in spite of the house of ill repute being operated upstairs, and a slick fellow in shirtsleeves and garters supplied Bretton with a cool beer without comment about his color. However, he just shook his head and moved off down the bar upon being questioned about a kid named Bledsoe.

Bretton propped his right boot on the rail for such, gulped some of the brew's foamy head, and scanned the room again in the mirror over the backbar. This place had more customers than where Tom was—most likely that was due to the bawdy women circulating the premises—yet none of the patrons caught Jonas's eye as having a likeness to the redheaded gunman. Still, he kept his rifle close.

Suddenly a buxom French lady loomed at his elbow. Her painted eyes said more than her words. "Lookin' for a good time, cowboy?"

Bretton had been among her sort in dives before, and he knew they generally had as much information stored about their customers as barkeepers did. So he met her sultry gaze and stated, "Naw, actually I'm in here huntin' a fella I know."

Before he could proceed, she chuckled and caressed his arm. "I have talked to many strong men, *cheri,* but never have they been looking for a fellow." Her come-on became bolder. "What say we go upstairs and have some fun, ah? If not with me, then perhaps one of my girls might strike your fancy. There's Beth, she has fine yellow skin and is eager to please."

Jonas shook his head. "Thanks anyhow. If I was lookin' for such, you'd do just fine. But I'm in a hurry. Do you know a Fast Bledsoe?"

The Frenchwoman patted his arm. "You're a flatterer. At least buy me a drink, *cheri.*"

Hoping it would bring him more success, Jonas conceded. She glanced around, wondered aloud and with irritation at the barman's absence, then took Bretton's coin and went over the counter to get it herself, revealing plenty of sensuous leg in the process. Back at the Negro's side, she lifted her glass of brandy in salute to him, and drained more than half.

"Now what about Bledsoe?" Jonas prompted. "Young fella, red hair, they say he's—"

"Sure, I know him. The boy, he's one of my best clients. Comes by every time he's in the area. He has a fondness for me.

"Why do you look for him, *cheri?*" She squared herself to him and eyed him with brazen thoroughness. "You can't be a lawman, too good-lookin'. . . . Ah, a bounty hunter perhaps?"

"No, ma'am, nothin' more glamorous than a hired hand for an outfit over on the Sabine." He wasn't going to be completely open, not just yet. "Ya knows he's a killer, then?"

"It is the way of men to brag in the company of women, especially paid women." For the first time she averted her gaze, and suddenly she did not appear so flirtatious. She downed the rest of her drink. "He always has plenty money. I know he is supposed to have killed several men. But so have many other gentleman, perhaps even you, *cheri.*"

Bretton ignored his beer; he was making headway. "But do ya know he's taken part in the murder of a woman and her little boy?" He saw surprise on her face then, and a hint of disgust. Therefore he hurried on, "That's right. I ride fo' the man whose family was torn up."

All the decency in her came to the surface suddenly. "He's sleepin' now in my private room."

Every nerve in Jonas Bretton stood on end and he clutched the madam's shoulders, bare and smooth above the revealing cut of her dress. "Tell me which one it is!"

Her intake of breath was sharp, and the tone she spoke in lost all seductiveness. "Second to the last at the end of the corridor up the stairs. On the right." As Bretton grabbed up his rifle and started to turn she added, "Be careful, *M'sieur.* He is very good with a gun!"

Bretton made no reply, and only now did the other people in the house pay any particular attention to him as he mounted the stairs two at a time. At the top a dim hallway lay before him. He went along it quickly but quietly, Winchester at the ready. When he reached the designated door at the line of shut cribs, he paused to listen and still himself.

A tremendous kick and rush and he was in the spacious chamber, pivoting and taking everything in, gun level at the waist and his body braced for a fight, maybe the shock of a bullet.

Nothing! Rumpled cover on the elaborate bed and the single window wide open. He strode forth to look outside, noticing a warbag lying in a corner. He didn't think that would be part of the French Woman's effects.

Crude stairs outside the window led to the trashy ground at the rear of the building. A fly buzzed around as Jonas pieced together the obvious in the stifling heat of the bedroom. Leaving the window and starting back the way he came, Jonas froze at a call from somewhere out front on the lone street.

"Cooper!"

No shots followed the sharp young voice like Jonas figured there would. Out into the hall and back down the stairway he rushed. In his haste he nearly bowled a couple over who were ascending to the cribs, yet Bretton didn't slow up. Going through the barroom at a jog, he saw the saloonkeeper again at his post. Jonas wanted to hurl a curse or a bullet at him—the snake had to be guilty of tipping off Bledsoe; it was plain in the fear now on his countenance—but Jonas didn't. Instead he concentrated on gaining the boardwalk and learning what the devil was going on outside.

Chapter Eleven

Tom Cooper had gotten nothing from the saloon proprietor who'd refused to serve Jonas, just that this was a live-and-let-live town and he didn't mix in other's affairs. So, downing the rest of the weak bourbon, Tom had walked out and up the street to the only mercantile.

The store was vacant of humans save a gray-haired man of middle age, with bushy black eyebrows, who rose from a straight chair by a stack of crates and took a dime from Tom and made change for the price of a cheroot he selected. Tom was in no mood to waste any more time with the people in this burg whom he'd come to think of as heathens, and soon as he got the slim, black cigar lit, he made plain his business.

Immediately the storekeeper's hands became uselessly busy with his apron and his face multiplied ten-fold in wrinkles. "Why you lookin' for Bledsoe?"

"That is strictly our concern. We'll take care of the business when we meet.

"But I happen to know he's in this hole in the road, and since it's obvious you know 'im, make it easy on us both and tell me where he's at. You'd be doin' society and yourself a big favor."

Despite having the counter between him and Tom, the clerk retreated a step. "W-wait a minute, Mister! I got no quarrel with you."

"And I none with you. *If* you'll be straight. I'm sure tired of gettin' the runaround from everybody!"

"Look, man, Fast Bledsoe ain't one for a guy to shoot his mouth off to a stranger about. Throwin' iron's how he got his name!"

"He'll not get your identity from me." Cooper stared hard through eyes narrowed against the layers of to-bacco smoke. "Now I'm waitin' to hear what ya know."

The fellow's lips moved. Nothing came out, so he cleared his throat and tried again. "I sell merchandise to ever'one that can pay the prices. I got no connection with the young devil 'cept that. I reckon he's stayin' with the madam of the cathouse up at Malloy's Palace. They're kinda close. That's all—"

Tom stood there no longer; he was out and headed toward the saloon Bretton was supposed to be in. Cooper was almost across the rutted street when his name was shouted, and he pivoted toward the little tavern he'd left only minutes ago. Bledsoe, smug and confident, was swaggering to meet him, his spurs adding to the scars on the edge of the sidewalk as he gained the dusty thoroughfare.

"I heard you and your hired hand was lookin' for me," the kid stated in a smart tone. "What's it all about that you'd ride so far? Ya look mighty trail-worn."

Cooper didn't like that the young killer kept coming right up to him, but he squared himself and stood spread-legged, hand near yet not touching the butt of his pistol, letting Bledsoe halt within six feet. Then he said loud enough for his voice to carry, "You killed my wife and boy, and now I'm here to get satisfaction."

Bledsoe's bright eyes flickered to the rooftops behind Tom, but returned quickly to the latter. "Y'all don't wantta tangle with me, Cooper. Trust me on that. Call your man out from wherever he's at, and we'll talk this over while havin' a drink."

Cooper clenched the rolled tobacco between his teeth in an attempt to bridle his murderous passion. "I wouldn't drink with you if it was my last chance at iced water 'fore an eternity in hell, you piece of trash."

Eyes could be felt on them from windows and sidewalks, and for an instant Cooper thought Fast Bledsoe was going to cut loose his wolf right then. But no, he

was a man who enjoyed such as this, an outlaw altogether unlike the bunch he rode with. Bledsoe was a
young man who thrived on the rush he got from facing
an opponent to kill or make slink away. Gunning a
fellow in an even break was exciting sport to him, a
way to build a reputation, nothing more or less.

He grinned. "Hard talk, Cooper. But I'm not the guy
ya want." Stoically he fingered Miguel and Zed for the
killings of Stan and Bell respectively.

"But you were there and didn't stop it!" retorted
Tom, straining to keep himself steady against the
waves of fury and hate that threatened to engulf him.

Bretton's easy voice, from behind and to the right:
"I'm on yo flank, Tom. And I'se got my sights lined
on that snake."

Now it was evident that that rankled the redhead,
but his gaze never faltered from Cooper and he talked
with increased excitement. "Hear tell you're handy
with a hogleg yourself, Cooper. Dusted a whole family
from over Louisiana way a few years back. That so?"

"Stand easy, Jonas," directed Tom, lifting his right
hand very slowly to remove the cheroot from his
mouth with all the casualness of a man on an afternoon
stroll. "I'm fair with a shootin' iron, boy. But I had
help with those Landises from a good ally, just like I
got from Jonas here with you and the rest of Rodel's
sorry bunch.

"Now, you let that gunbelt fall and give it up.

You're gonna hang just like the woman-and-child killer you are." Even as he gambled, Tom knew the risk he took, what with his hand so far from his Colt. Yet it was that very fact he figured would cause the kid gunman to become more confident and lose his edge. And it did.

"The man don't live that can take my gun." Although Bledsoe kept alert, he laughed outright. "Hang? I may die right here, but I won't *hang*. How much you wantta bet I can get lead into you both 'fore your man ever plugs me?" The fingers of his gun hand twitched like the tail of a disturbed rattler.

Indeed it had been a great while since Tom had been called on to draw his revolver with speed. When was the last time he'd even fired it? Not that the conversion to metal cartridges had ever proved the 1860 Army unreliable, as it had some others—not even once had it misfired. What concerned Cooper now was his own ability opposed to this youngster who was supposed to be so fast.

Always he'd known fear when going against another man, however. It wouldn't overcome him though, for every man faced the possibility of his own mortality before going into battle, at least those who are rational do. And actually, the reason he chose to go about it in another fashion than straight-up was not the chance of death itself, but the fact that to be dead would keep him from getting to Rodel. That, plus he wanted to show this kid his gun *could* be taken, and he *would* stretch hemp.

All this time he had been holding the cigar poised before his lips, and now he rejuvenated the dying tip with a couple of nonchalant puffs, seeing the surety in Bledsoe gradually dissolve and anger grow as he flicked away ash and let the tense moment linger another little bit.

It was extremely hot in the sunny street, the kind of hot that can make a man weak. From some shade cast by a building a wren twittered over her nest in the rafters of an awning. Sweat beaded on the opposing factions as time stood still on this scalding day.

With a thump of his second finger Cooper sent the burning ember arcing toward Bledsoe's shirtfront. Involuntarily, the kid brought up both hands to parry the stub of tobacco coal. Tom Cooper stepped forward then with a straight left to the mouth, his right hand, now empty, dipping for the grip of his Army Colt. Fast Bledsoe sat down hard, blood on his lips, and by the time the glazed look left him, Cooper had him disarmed and jerked to his feet. He pushed the muzzle of his revolver into Bledsoe's midsection and told Jonas to bind his hands using the outlaw's own belt.

Bretton uttered while obeying, "Lord, I thought y'all would never make a play!" Everything had been peculiarly acute to him while he kept the sights of his repeater centered on Bledsoe—the killer's expression, the dialogue between him and Tom, citizens giving room but gawking with morbid curiosity natural to the human race, right down to the boisterous racket down at the sawmill.

Tom commanded him to fetch one of their mounts and Jonas did so, leading his blond sorrel over to where Tom marched the kid up under a lamppost in front of the smaller saloon. In the rope coiled on the saddle horn Cooper made a loop, stating the prisoner had best ask his Maker for forgiveness, because none was coming from the head of the family whom he'd slain. Seemingly dozens of men and women appeared from nowhere to crowd around, and Bledsoe's light complexion turned a pale shade of green as he suddenly knew true fear.

He turned first one way then the other, in search of a face friendly enough to heed his imploring words to save him from these two lynchers. For God's sake, this was murder!

As rebuttal to the kid's pleas, Tom gave loudly the testimony of what Bledsoe and his cronies had done at the Cooper homestead and that of the Hadzlots. Jonas backed up the story and roughly boosted the redhead into the saddle amid angry concurrences from the multitude to proceed with the execution. What friends Bledsoe had in the throng of townspeople weren't on good enough terms to buck this; most of those who had protected him had done so out of fear or self-gain.

Jonas watched Tom prepare the hang rope over a crossbar of the lamppost and around the neck of the condemned, and he felt a blood lust akin to Cooper's. Sure, there was a coldness in him at what they were doing, but it wasn't remorse. It was more a worry of what they might have to face when the authorities learned of it. Yet . . . this *was* justice, quick and sure, no matter what the law read.

Never before had Fast Luke Bledsoe been scared like this; the mare he sat was excited, and her nervous movements made the noose tighten around his throat. He told himself to be calm. He still had a hole card, if only . . .

The kid bought time with talk as he wrestled inconspicuously with his bonds. "I tell you it's Zed ya want, and I can tell ya how to find 'im!"

Cooper had been about to signal Bretton to start the horse from beneath Bledsoe, yet now halted. "Go ahead. But make it quick."

"Yeah, him and the Injun," Bledsoe began, licking dry lips, "they're up to his hideout on the Neches. Go north on this road till you come to the second fork, not the one headed back to the ferry on the Angelina. Take the left branch, and it'll lead right into the Neches bottom."

The young gunman found it difficult not to allow

his straining against the belt around his wrists show as he continued, slowly, "Four or five miles on, a dim lane leads off to the south. It's hard to see, a growed-up freighting road is all it is. Anyhow, 'fore long it parallels a little creek and runs due west. You'll—"

At that instant the kid got his girlish but deadly right hand free and someone in the crowd gave a warning shout—too late. A flick of the wrist brought a two-shot derringer from his sleeve and into play. It spat at Cooper, and the sandy-haired man felt the sharp pain of its small-caliber bite, yet he grabbed iron with little or no hesitation.

Jonas gave a whoop and slapped the sorrel on the rump soon as he saw the short, silver barrels. Bledsoe's legs tightened on the mount instinctively and his left spur caught in the cinch while he made a try at putting his last bullet in the black man. A .44 slug from Tom's Army Colt ripped into the redhead's guts just then and played havoc with Bledsoe's shot; it buzzed by Jonas's ear like a river-bottom mosquito. And then it was over.

Almost before Fast Bledsoe's brain could register he'd been hit, his thought processes were shut down for good. Anchored to the crude gallows by the lasso, his neck snapped audibly when his body stretched to the limit by the horse charging forth with his foot hung in the saddle rigging. If his boot hadn't come off, no doubt he would have been decapitated, but thus released, he swung free with his neck lengthened to the point his toes nearly brushing the dusty street. Gasps, exclamations, and hoofbeats filled the air. Dust, blood, and powder smoke burned Bretton's nose.

He swore and rushed to Tom's side. During the set-to the bystanders had scattered away from the gunplay, and now they thronged back in to have a good look, commenting on what they had just witnessed, and the outcome. Cooper hunkered on his knees and let Jonas examine his punctured thigh. It took only a glance to see that the ball, likely a .32, was still in his person. All Cooper knew right then was that they had gotten one of his quarries—and he hurt like the devil. But lead he'd taken before, and he said as much.

A gent with a ruddy face stooped over him and jerked a thumb toward the limp corpse. "Same should be done to all woman-and-child killers. What you need, friend, is a doctor. There's one got an office down by the mill yonder."

Cooper gritted his teeth and stood with most of his weight on his left leg. Knowing the slug should be extracted by a skilled hand, he nodded, and Bretton and the citizen, along with a few others, ushered him along toward the noise of the sawmill and the local physician.

For ten full minutes a bewhiskered codger with spectacles and a Swedish accent dug for the piece of lead with a lengthy metal probe. Cooper clenched his teeth, grunted, cursed, and tried not to writhe on the none-too-soft operating table. The screech of the saws and the yelling of men to each other and the work stock bringing in logs at the mill further increased his misery, and he wondered why in tarnation a place of rest and healing had been positioned so close to such a riotous area.

Directly, the serious pain let up as the doc stepped back with as much sweat on him as Tom, but the latter took notice that the sawbones deposited no slug in the waiting pan of antiseptic.

"I cannot get it," the physician declared.

The whole time Bretton had been restless to one side of the little room, silent but nervous, and now he found his tongue. "What do you mean? Ya got to!"

"I don't got to do anythin' that is impossible," returned the doc with obvious indignation. "For thirty-five years I have been a doctor, and I should know when a bullet is too deep! This town, it has more broken bones, stabbings, and gunshot vounds brought to me than all other illnesses put together with childbearing!"

The elder babbled a mite at the amount of violence in the world, then inhaled deeply and turned to his patient who had raised up on one elbow. "It is in the bone of the thigh. It is a vonder it didn't break the bone in two. You must stay here until I can make sure infection von't set in. I vill—"

Cooper's speech was short though even. "Forget it. I got business to tend. Bandage me up and I'll be outta here."

Frowning, the old Swede explained, "Sir, men can sometimes live long time vith lead inside them, but only if the vound heals around it properly. Here you need to be, vhere I can vatch it close. It will have to be amputated if blood poisonin' sets in."

Cooper growled he knew about what a killer gangrene was—he'd been in the War—then demanded to have the wound wrapped up. Bretton stepped forward and suggested, "You stay with the doc, Tom. I'll go on after Rodel."

A couple of citizens had filled the doctor in on what this had come up about when Tom had been deposited in his office, and he urged while swabbing the raw hole with a fiery liquid, "Yes, listen to your friend, Cooper. Ridin' vill not help you or your cause."

Tom Cooper's mouth was a firm line. "I won't ask a man to do what I can't. It's my responsibility. If I can just get on the trail, I won't need to live but a few more days, anyway.

"Now, Jonas, go get our horses and fetch me my extra pair of jeans to replace these. Sawbones, you just patch me the best ya can, you hear? But I don't want any more advice!"

Silence in the humid office, save for the irritating din of the mill next door, but both men obeyed the orders. Mind spinning with worry, Bretton strode outside and found that some good Samaritan had brought Tom's and his own mount up and tied them before the building. Although it was getting on in the afternoon, it wasn't cooling off in the least. If anything, it was hotter now than at midday.

He noticed a big man coming from the heart of the little town on a swift-footed bronc, but he didn't recognize him, and thought nothing of it as he dug in Tom's saddlebags for the requested pants. The rider came on down the street, however, and drew rein by him on his tough-looking horse and stepped down.

Off the cayuse the fellow didn't look nearly so big, in fact he was much shorter than Jonas. Yet the stranger, barrel-chested with strong arms and lean hips, was nonetheless formidable. Jonas quickly got the impression from the way he was being studied that the gent wasn't here for the doc's services, so he turned to face him.

"Somethin' I can do?"

The guy knuckled back a walrus mustache on his deeply lined face. "Maybe. You Bretton, ride for a man by the name of Tom Cooper?"

Jonas inclined his head. "Sho am. Why?" Plenty whites still didn't like being questioned by a black man, but Bretton wasn't afraid. If he'd been the type to scare easily, he wouldn't be about his and Tom's present business.

Revealing a small, encircled star pinned to his shirt beneath a grey vest, the man stated, "Folks up at the saloon where that fella's strung up said I'd find y'all down here. I'm Lonny Oates, Texas Ranger."

Chapter Twelve

Oates had been one step behind Tom and Jonas ever since San Augustine, and now he was brought up to date while Cooper was being patched. The Ranger reprimanded the pair of vigilantes, then asserted he would handle it from here out. Cooper blandly stated he'd continue on, all the same, and paid the physician for his services.

The Swedish doctor graciously offered the trio to stay there in private and talk things out for themselves while he went to check on a patient just out of town. Prior to leaving them in his office, he shook his head at Cooper's determination and handed him a container of salve with the advice to: "Keep that vound clean and packed vith this, above all else you do."

"Look, Cooper, you—" Oates began soon as they were alone.

Tom was too worked up to sit still and stood leaning on his Spencer Jonas had brought him to use as a cane. He interrupted the Ranger, "Don't start preachin' to me! I been on those devils' trail ever since the stage robbery, and I won't back off now 'cause some lawman who just arrived tells me to. We're wastin' valuable time. I done told ya what Bledsoe said!"

Oates bristled. "I represent the state, Mister, and have been assigned to this job by Headquarters. It's what I do for a living, huntin' badmen, and you got no business in this anymore. I could arrest you for what ya did a little while ago!"

Jonas didn't like the way his friend retorted, "Go ahead." Was there a challenge in it?

"Let's be reasonable." Jones stepped forward to maybe prevent something very bad. "Oates, we mebbe broke the law, but you can be certain justice was served up yonder in the street. Now we done told ya what we learned from that murderin' kid, and it sho be dangerous fo' one man to go a-ridin' into that hideout alone. Why don't ya jes' deputize us to go with ya?"

Inhaling deeply, Lonny Oates rubbed a sleeve across his rugged face and said, "Fast Luke Bledsoe was wanted dead or alive in Galveston, and if I arrest y'all I oughtta take half this town into custody with ya.

"But head home, I tell you. I'm used to this, and a couple of amateurs, not to mention one that's wounded, will only slow me down.

"Heck, you don't even know that Bledsoe wasn't just shootin' his mouth off to buy some time before goin' for that sneak gun!"

"I ain't no greenhorn at gunplay!" declared Cooper. "As for this leg, when it starts holdin' you back I'll say nothing 'bout being left behind." He raised his voice for emphasis. "Till then, our destinations are the same because we've got no reason to believe Bledsoe lied. So we can all head that way together, or in separate groups."

Realizing the futility of another try at getting Tom to stay behind to attend his injury, Jonas Bretton added, "It's up to you, Oates, but I think you'd feel better backed by two more guns."

The square-built lawman had a habit of standing hipshot with his left hand resting on the butt of the .45 Peacemaker belted just below and to the left of his navel—its short, nickel-plated barrel pointed at an angle toward his right leg—and he shifted his weight, apparently digesting this ultimatum. Abruptly and with a frown he consented and swore them in with a few brief words. There were no badges to give them; they were not true Rangers, anyway, only possemen sworn to help in the apprehension of Zed Rodel and Choctaw Blue.

Tom refused aid in getting aboard his mustang, ignoring the pain at the core of his right thigh, glad it wasn't the other leg and that the horse wasn't as tall as the blond mare Jonas rode. He sat the coal-black horse in front of the general store while Oates and Bretton went in and got provisions. He was not in a good mood, body *or* soul, and he kept his mouth shut on the way back through Malloy abreast of the other two at a canter. Action was what he wanted, not useless palaver.

Bledsoe no longer dangled back there from the lamppost. Oates had ordered the cadaver cut down and buried in the community's boot hill, ending the fun of the children who'd been entertaining themselves chucking dirt clods at it and poking it with sticks. The young killer's demise would go in the Ranger's report when this was all over with. He'd sought for Bledsoe's share of the loot in all the young man's belongings, in the hotel room and at the livery, but no more money was found save the few coins in his pockets. Very likely one of the kid's acquaintances had cleaned out the dirty stash right after learning of his death.

Each of the trio was mounted well, and Oates's mouse-colored pony struck Tom as fine stock. To his experienced eye it appeared to perhaps have some Morgan or other good ancestry mixed with its native blood. This only reminded him of working on the Louisiana horse ranch where he had made the stake which gave him and Bell their start . . . now this. After only six years together!

A tense surliness draped each individual in the little posse. None of them spoke, intent on covering ground before nightfall. And so they did, halting several miles beyond the first fork they were to come to, where Bledsoe had split away from his saddle partners to go to Malloy.

In the tasks of making camp in the dark they uttered their first words since leaving the sawmill town. Jonas saw to the horses, and Oates went about getting supper. Tom couldn't do much labor, yet he insisted on refilling their canteens and fetching water for coffee down at a small creek on the side of the red-oak knoll they had settled on. Then he examined his wound by the firelight.

It was red, tender, and he could tell he had a slight fever. Although that was normal for a short while after most any gunshot wound. He stuffed the hole with the salve the doc gave him, felt it burn down deep, and tied on a fresh dressing.

Above the incessant chirping of crickets hissed the bacon the Ranger shaved into a hot skillet with a Bowie knife. Bretton returned from the picketed horses to help him mix up and put on enough biscuits for supper and leftovers to eat on the move the next day. As it all cooked, Jonas queried about Tom's leg. Cooper grunted that it was all right and occupied himself with a cigarette until the meal was done, feeling anxious and uncomfortable, every now and then pitching a twig into the flames.

Supper passed in total quietness, save for the natural sounds of a camp in the forest; each man's brain was as busy as his digestive system. Every individual always had their own thoughts and concerns, and at such a hard task, this group was heavily laden with both.

Oates cleared his throat and rubbed a sleeve across his mouth after draining his cup for the second time. "Just so nobody's mistaken, I want you boys to know this game will be played exactly how I say."

Tom fired back, "Us *boys* don't consider this a game!"

"Dang it, Cooper, ya know what I meant! Rodel's a bad *hombre,* and most likely him and that Injun'll fight to the death. In which case it'll be shoot straight or die, but still y'all will follow my orders!

"Should we take one or both alive they'll be escorted back to Maple Springs for trial. Sure as shootin' there'll be no necktie party till a judge and jury says so. And they'll say so, have no doubt."

Tom Cooper offered neither yea nor nay but just lay back, shifted his throbbing leg, and covered his eyes with his hat. He was glad Oates didn't press for agreement with his way of thinking, for it would have precipitated an argument.

Justice was not a sure thing in the courts, Cooper knew all too well. A fellow he'd worked with in Louisiana, who was guilty of nothing more serious than getting a bit liquored up on payday, had been sentenced to five years at a penitentiary in Baton Rouge for a holdup he did not commit. The guy had been one of Tom's few friends right after coming South, and in spite of Tom's truthful testimony to his innocence, he was found guilty.

And on the reverse side, Cooper had witnessed the court-martialing of a fellow cavalryman for desertion in combat during the War. The indictment was irrevocably valid, yet the coward got off with dishonorable discharge instead of execution, simply because his father was a respected officer in the Army of the Potomac.

First-hand memories such as these, plus other stories he had heard of, made Cooper dubious of allowing the situation to be handled by anyone other than himself. At the same time, he didn't relish the idea of being at odds with a Texas Ranger. Pondering this and what lay ahead tomorrow, it was quite late before the hurt man slept.

Jonas refused the lawman's help in cleaning the dishes. He silently cursed the Ranger's arrival. Also, he was aggravated by his friend's stubbornness at disregarding his health. Blast it all!

Jonas knew Tom well enough to know he wouldn't give up short of death, and he feared both that, and a physical clash between Tom and the Ranger.

Rodel and Blue were encamped without a fire that same night in a small hollow just back from the little stream which paralleled the almost-indistinct freight road leading to the hideout on the Neches. They had not pushed themselves hard since separating from Bledsoe, yet they had made fair time because Zed knew the route so well. Otherwise, it would be difficult for one to stick to the dim trace which had been obliterated through the years.

Here, just three miles up from the shack built on stilts down in the bottom on the bank of an oxbow lake, Rodel intended to wait on Bledsoe and make sure trouble was off their back trail for good.

"We're gonna be hungry 'fore Fast gets here with supplies," Blue thought aloud while chewing his part of the remaining jerky. "*If* the little snake gets here. I don't trust the peckerwood."

Zed drank thoughtfully from his canteen. "I'll stand watch tomorrow while you ride on to the shack and bring back the cans of beans and tomatoes I keep there. That'll hold us for a while."

He had the same misgivings about the kid gunman

as the breed did, however. To his Indian companion he allowed how Fast Bledsoe was one to get carried away by a good time. He was cocky, and he'd want to strut some for that French fancy lady he cottoned to in Malloy. Carousing and glory-hunting were downfalls of the kid's.

If he *did* return with the ordered provisions, Zed would let the Choctaw have his way with him. Still, Rodel really figured, by the kid remarking he wanted to go it alone, that they had seen the last of Fast Bledsoe.

The flaxen-haired outlaw told himself all was better with just Blue. For the present. Others could be recruited to his gang once things settled down again.

Would things settle down?

He muttered an obscenity after Blue moved off to stand the first watch. Never had he had such a doubt; the half-breed's worry must have rubbed off on him. Zed Rodel had lived by his wits for over twenty years as an owl hoot, and in that span he'd never become weak in the knees after something he had done.

Although Blue did have a legitimate point—abuse of women was not tolerated by plenty, even many notorious killers of men.

And Cooper had been in that San Augustine posse.

Rodel shook his head. What difference did it make? There had been other vengeful friends and relatives of his victims, and they had all been overcome one way or another. Not to mention Zed had never spent one minute as a prisoner in any kind of jail. It wasn't as though Cooper's woman and that little foreign gal had been the first of the fair sex he had treated roughly.

Without any thunder or lightning at all, it began to drizzle, and Zed rolled up in his poncho atop his groundsheet, knowing Blue would awake him around midnight for his turn at guard duty. In his life Rodel guessed he had killed somewhere close to a dozen people, probably more. He did not keep count because he just didn't care. Unlike Bledsoe, Zed was the type of criminal who graded how well he was doing by how full his pockets were, not how many people he could beat in a duel. Killing was just a necessity sometimes if you wanted wealth.

Yes, Zed Rodel had killed, and he tried to console himself with the fact he could surely kill some more to continue looking out for his own interest. . . . Nevertheless, a bad feeling nagged at him, something he was not at all accustomed to. He didn't like it.

At the crack of dawn Choctaw Blue started his contrary mule down off the sandy knoll about their camp toward the hideout, a cigarette aglow between his thin lips. The temptation of fogging it out of the country was great as he surrounded the little oxbow lake circled by willows and cypresses. But he didn't, and returned to Rodel with the canned goods from the shanty sitting atop a high but narrow terrace between river and lake.

He'd keep his guns handy and stick with Zed; didn't the money in his grip prove it was worth it? The older man was slick. Going into Bentosa well dressed and with blackened hair to nose around in preparation for the stage job proved that.

Of course, it was a dangerous life. Then again, so were many kinds of honest work. And the latter sure didn't pay as much.

Chapter Thirteen

Pain, throbbing and persistent, had kept Tom awake
for the last two hours before Jonas and the Ranger rose
from their blankets to get ready for the new day. That
intense darkness prior to dawn lay over the forest
while Oates built up the fire and put on grits, bacon,
and coffee. By the time Jonas saddled the three horses
and brought them up close, Tom had washed and
changed the bandage on his wound and breakfast was
done. It was only after they ate that the first words
were spoken by any of them.

"Gotta be on the move," Oates asserted stiffly, dous-
ing the fire with the leavings in the coffeepot.

Bretton grunted concurrence, but Cooper said nothing, shaking his head at his friend's offer to boost him
onto the black gelding. Tom didn't want the other two

146

men to know his condition was worsening—his leg was swollen and much more inflamed this morning—and he clenched his teeth at swinging the appendage awkwardly over the cantle to the off stirrup. He knew he was being scrutinized in the increasing light as they all reined back to the road and continued north.

Every jolt of the ride that day was torture for the wounded man. He tried to keep most of his weight on the left leg, letting the right hang loose as possible, yet on some of the hilly terrain he had to shift himself contrary to his comfort to assist the mustang on the unlevel ground.

Seldom was anything said, and what *was* pertained strictly to their route, the lack or age of sign, and the progress they made. An occasional homestead was passed as they rode steadily along the trace; around midday Lonny Oates questioned a couple traveling in a buckboard as to whether they had seen any horsemen of Rodel and Blue's descriptions. Negative, and the man laid his rifle across his lap and thanked the posse for the warning before slapping the lines on the rump of his harnessed nag.

At the second fork in the wagon road, they turned left as Bledsoe had directed and felt some better about the truth of the gunman's story. Indeed this strand of the highway angled northwest, down off the uplands between the Angelina and Neches Valleys. Grades of broken rock and sand were picked over and around.

In some areas the horses' hooves sank deeply in the damp sand. It had rained here last night, and whatever tracks might have been made prior to that were a hopeless case now. Too, the continuous ascent and descent were tiresome on man and beast. It wasn't a pleasant day, to say the least.

Jonas Bretton could read through Cooper's stoic front. The man was hurting, it was obvious. At times he'd wince, at others he would seem to be in a daze, and Jonas feared he might fall from his seat. He shoved on in silence with his companions—he wished not to talk with Oates at all, and he knew Cooper should be left to himself and his troubles.

Tom was a good fellow, a better friend couldn't be found, although he was hard and stubborn. Bretton remembered hearing Bell comment that once he set himself at something, only death or the Almighty's intervention could stop him. Thus Bretton walked his bronc alongside that of his friend, ready to help him in any way, worrying all the while.

Somewhere about five miles further on, a dim trail wound away to the west. The trio took to it, ducking the low limbs of post oak and blackjack which arched overhead, bluestem grass rubbing their mounts' bellies. Soon the path sloped down at a sharp angle to parallel the brook Bledsoe had spoken of. Here the trail widened quite a bit, and Oates got down to examine something.

"We'll pull over into that chaparral yonder and halt till mornin'," he decided abruptly.

Bretton queried, "What'd you find?"

"Horse droppings. 'Bout two days old, no more'n that. Been grazin' wild."

"Heck, it ain't dark! Let's go on." Cooper was even more anxious now, for he did not feel well at all. He wanted to get on with it; he'd begun to fear he would die before he saw this through. During the day the effects of blood poisoning had become obvious to him.

"We've gotta be gettin' close to their hideout," Oates said firmly. "We're dropping down into the river bottom now. We'll stay the night *here*. Not more'n a hour of good light left, and I sure don't wantta start something they might get out of under the cover of darkness. Do you?"

Tom shook his head and objected no more as they entered a cluster of young pin oaks and French mulberries back from the stream, and Jonas was truly glad. He recognized his comrade's need for rest in full when Tom staggered upon dismounting in a scant opening that would be their campsite in the dense brush. However, Jonas saw him steady himself against the mustang and resisted the urge to rush to his side.

A man like Tom needed all the independence he could manage. It was just his way.

The tiny clearing was on the side of a steep hill which descended to the branch bottom and was barely sufficient in size for the small posse and their animals. Yet it was secluded, and relatively safe because of that. Since there was a decent chance they were closing in on the quarry, however, Lonny Oates asserted there would be no fire and supper would consist of hardtack. Cooper, though he didn't like it, allowed Jonas to strip his gelding for him while he, slowly and with his weight on his left leg and the butt of the Spencer, sat down and took care of his wound on the blankets he scattered haphazardly.

The dressing he removed was severely stained with corruption, and the application of the salve to the raw hole after it was washed very nearly took his breath. He hurried to bandage it again before the other men might see the wound, and he silently condemned the piece of buried lead that was gradually taking his strength, his life.

Accepting a portion of jerked beef and tough bread, Cooper ate very little of it. The other two noticed this, glanced at each other, and for the first time Jonas knew the Ranger was truly concerned over Tom's well-being. It was Jonas who could no longer hold silent the wish that he'd turn back for medical help.

Waves of mist seemed to cloud Tom's mind every now and then, and it was a lengthy interval which passed before he formed the words: "Too late for that. I just wantta take those devils out with me."

Oates pulled his canteen away from a grim mouth. "That ain't no way to talk, Cooper."

"By God, it is from my point of view! Those heathens caused me to bury my whole family! And they sure have made sorrow for the survivors of many another poor victim!"

Bretton shared the burst of his friend's temper. "Don't be talkin' right and wrong to us, Mister Ranger! We seen first-hand the destruction Rodel can leave—I thank God that Bell Cooper wasn't left a shattered hull like that little Hadzlot girl—so don't be a-preachin' to us!

"The Almighty didn't mean fo' devils like them to walk the face of this earth without opposition. That's why he's created ways of stoppin' 'em." He tapped a long, dark finger on the stock of his '73 Winchester.

A deathly quiet pervaded suddenly. One of the horses blew nervously at the tension in the air. The lawman corked his canteen and set it down, his gaze on the light-brown sand between his boots. With a deep breath he rose from the hunk of limestone he'd been seated on and took up his usual hipshot, hand-on-Colt stance.

After slewing his gaze around at the growing dusk and rubbing his lengthy mustache, he said sincerely, "We got off on the wrong foot from the start, and that's bad. I can understand the way y'all feel, I sure can."

"How do you reckon that?" Tom demanded gruffly.

"A long time ago, when I was just sixteen, I lived with my family on a poor little spread just this side of El Paso," he began without preamble. "It was a rough country, and still is.

"Anyhow, that spring, a renegade of Mexican and Apache blood came over the river from Juarez and attacked a young lady on the Texas side. She was a pretty, smart little thing who helped her pa in his general store every day. The outlaw killed her father and did as he pleased with her after breakin' into the store one night for provisions. Nothing could be learned from the traumatized girl, but an eye witness fingered the culprit and set the law in the right direction.

"The young lady, she died the following afternoon under a doctor's care, whatever life she'd had ahead of her snuffed out 'fore it got good started."

He shifted his husky frame so his weight was on the other foot. "That girl, she was a cousin of mine that I'd courted since New Year's Eve."

Here he paused for a spell, and Cooper brought out the makings from his shirt pocket. His hands trembled so badly more tobacco was spilled than hit the tiny paper and he gave up the project. He looked back to the Texas Ranger as he continued the story.

Every able-bodied man in the Oates clan, along with plenty of neighbors and friends, came to the call of a posse. The rogue half-breed quit the country, though, and skillfully lost them in the rough country of New Mexico. The sheriff gave it up after three futile days and ordered everybody home.

Oates declared, "The formal posse was disbanded, but the manhunt was still on as far as me and several others were concerned. Over a week we roamed hard country up the Rio Grande, keepin' our eyes peeled and questioning ever'one we came across. Way into the Sonoran Desert on the *Jornada del Muerto* we finally got a break.

"A dry-farming peon knew of the fella we sought, said he had a little hut down in a pocket canyon near the river. He offered to guide us and we took 'im up on it."

Spitting as if to rid himself of a bitter taste, Oates wiped a sleeve over his mouth and redistributed his weight once again. "To make a long story short, we captured the half-breed by force in a hell-raisin' scrap. None of us was of a mind to haul him all the way back to Texas and a judge, so with a rawhide *reata* and a gnarled cottonwood we carried out our own brand of justice."

"Then you *do* know how it feels," Jonas surmised in a low tone.

"I sure do."

Cooper asked, "So you'll let us do the same if Rodel and the Choctaw are caught?"

"No." Tom cursed and Oates raised his hands.

"Now hear me out! I done some rough stuff before joinin' the Rangers, maybe some of it would mark me as an outlaw. But now I ride for this." He pointed to the badge on his chest. "I took an oath to get it, and the way I see things, all a man has in the world sometimes is his strength and his word.

"Now I ain't sayin' whichever way Rodel's dealt with is right or wrong, or if there's even a tinker's damn worth of difference. But I'll say this: Till the day I resign from the Texas Rangers, I'll see things done by the book."

Cooper pushed his pain- and anger-filled haze aside completely for the first time. And he remembered taking that vow with Jonas by Oates back in that sawmill town. With a level gaze at both men, he stated, "I won't live to see the trial if we apprehend 'em, so I'll leave it to y'all to see justice done for my wife and boy, and all the other poor victims.

"When I go, one of you get the envelope of papers inside my vest. See to 'em, Jonas. They pertain to business matters." Without anything more he reclined and rolled up in his blankets, chilly from fever in spite of the night's heat.

Another furtive but meaning look passed between Oates and Bretton then, and the shocking reality of Tom's failing health hit Jonas like a hammer. Never had he seen any ailment or injury hold his friend back. It was Cooper's decision, of course, and he'd made it.

Yet under his breath Jonas cursed the stubbornness that would cause him to lose his boss and *taysha.*

All was dangerously serious in the world now; no light-hearted moments seemed to have ever existed, nor would any ever again. A whippoorwill called and the mournful sound increased Bretton's gloom as he lay back with melancholy thoughts.

Darkness was full by now, and inky forms were all that could be seen of men, animals, and inanimate objects. Insects hummed or chirped, a bullfrog gave his deep resonant croak. Further toward the river to the west a barred owl hooted.

A twig snapped close by and the lawman's grulla snorted loudly. Oates was making for the ebony lump which was his bedroll when this met his ears and instantly he was in a crouch, the Peacemaker in his left hand, its short barrel pointed up and the hammer at half-cock. What little starlight reached the campsite glimmered faintly on the weapon.

A split second later Jonas was coming to his knees, grabbing for the rifle by his blankets. "What was that?"

The straining eyes of the Ranger couldn't penetrate the obscurity of the encircling thicket, and he faded off into it after saying, "Don't know. Cover the stock."

It took Tom Cooper until then to get into a seated position and pick up his carbine. His movements were slow; the hefty long gun felt awkward and clumsy in his weak hands. In disgust he discarded it for the easier-handled Colt Army. Hoarsely he told Jonas to move over by the mounts, nervous on their tethers.

Bretton did so, keeping low and soothing first one, then another horse with a touch or word, his muscles like taut fencing wire until Oates strode back into view shaking his head.

"Must've been a coyote or some other varmint. I'll take a better look around come first light." He returned the .45 to its holster and picked up his Henry rifle. Checking the load in the chamber, he concluded, "We'll keep a tight guard tonight. I'll take the first watch and Bretton can take the last."

Cooper watched Lonny Oates disappear into the bleak shadows around the small camp and didn't argue over not having a shift at sentry duty. Ordinarily, he would have, because he was one to carry his own share of the load, if not more. At the present, though, he felt everyone would be safer with the other two on watch. He could hardly keep his eyes open.

Chapter Fourteen

Late that same evening, just a half-hour before twilight, after the pair of outlaws had finished a supper of tomatoes and beans right out of the cans, the Choctaw beseeched Rodel to let him scout their back trail. "That lyin' Bledsoe ain't comin', and I'd feel better with a look-see," he announced. "We gotta stay on our toes."

Zed returned with a thoughtful nod, "Go take a gander. But don't be all night."

The Indian removed his spurs hurriedly and rose from the pine log they had dragged up to sit on. "I'll do better afoot than on that sorry mule." And he departed with revolver and knife, leaving his single-shot carbine behind.

Rodel was restless, and not a little uneasy. Waiting

vigilantly for both friend and foe was getting to him. Was the absence of Bledsoe of the swaggering kid's own accord? Or had something happened to him?

For some reason the widowed Cooper and his hired nigger worried Zed Rodel.

That worry in turn vexed the outlaw leader tremendously. Since when did he allow a seed of anxiety to germinate in himself over absolutely anything to such an extent as this? Always he'd been carefree, holding the world and everyone in it in contempt. Yet, the memory of Tom Cooper charging off that ridge east of the Attoyac on his solid-black horse to aid in the rescue of that crippled boy . . . well, that vision conjured the idea of an avenging angel.

Was he still coming?

Just then Rodel cursed himself profanely for being soft in the head. If he showed a yellow streak, Blue would go back to fearing reprisal for what they had done. And realistically, once a fellow's guts became hollow, he was worthless in any kind of a scrap— generally he never regained his courage. Zed would never get anywhere in his work should he show the white feather now.

He adjusted his hat, swatted at a persistent mosquito, and went to move the mounts in closer from where they had been picketed all day in reach of grass and water at the edge of the shallow stream. Seated again on the deadfall, he awaited Blue's return in the swiftly growing darkness, alert, and with the greener across his knees. Time dragged.

It was a couple of hours later when the Indian materialized from the dark woods. He strode directly up to Zed and he was just a silhouette to the latter.

"They're back there, camped no more'n four miles," said Blue, low and tersely.

"Good, that's good, real good." A cool steadiness was suddenly upon Rodel, and he caressed the high hammers of the shotgun, chuckling to himself at the doubt he'd had during the wait.

"No," insisted his companion, "it sure *ain't* good! Zed, there's a Texas Ranger with Cooper and the black man! There was enough light left when I got to their camp for me to see his badge good. He nearly caught me when I stepped on a twig, come right by me in a thicket, and I saw him but he didn't see me." That encircled star which symbolized the state law really scared Blue, and it showed in the pitch of his voice.

He went on, "Zed, ya start buckin' the Rangers and you've got trouble, *bad* trouble! I heard 'em talking and they'll be comin' at good light. Cooper's got hurt somehow, but they'll be on us in no time."

"Hear 'em say anythin' about knowing how close we are?"

"No, so I think we oughtta get a move on!"

"Hellfire, calm down, will ya? We got it just like

we want it. We know when they're coming and we'll be waitin' at that little glade upstream a ways."

"But we ain't got much ammunition!" The Choctaw was perplexed at Rodel's cool air. "We—"

"Shut up and *listen!* Bledsoe must've run out on us, so it's up to me and you from here on out. True, we don't have a lotta shells. But you don't need many for a dry gulch.

"So that's how we'll play it. Then we can move on without bein' hounded. There's only three of 'em. Put 'em down quick, and we can go over on the Trinity. Got some friends down there that'll take care of us."

Choctaw Blue took a long, slow breath as Rodel stood. "Well, if we're gonna do it, wouldn't it be better to ease back there and hit 'em while they're asleep? They didn't have no fire, and I could probably get in close enough for knife work."

Zed considered this shortly, then shook his head. "Don't wantta run the chance of one of 'em gettin' away in the dark. We'll let 'em come to us and make a clean sweep. Be like shooting a coon in a butter churn.

"Relax about the Ranger. Hear? No matter what kinda law he is, a bullet in the brain will dust 'im like it will any livin' thing.

"Now c'mon! Let's get the horses and move into position. By noon tomorrow we'll have clear sailin' with all this cash!"

At the edge of the clearing, with the animals saddled and ready back in some hollies, the two men hunkered down. The open expanse before them lay quiet and dusky, knee-high grass swaying softly in a scant breeze beneath two leaning sugar maples which offered the only real cover for quite a span. The narrow stream ran along its sandy bed to their left, with very few shrubs and vines along its banks, not even a rock big enough for a man to take shelter behind. Rodel took all this in and smiled.

Blue sat against a pitch-pine stump and began to feel better after examining the terrain and hearing out some more reassuring words from Zed; the latter swore to put a bullet into the redheaded kid who'd run out on them, if they ever met up again. Once this little confrontation was dealt with in the morning, Zed predicted that their string of bad luck would be over.

Blue checked the single .52 cartridge in his Sharps carbine and felt of the three remaining loads in the loops of his cartridge belt next to perhaps a dozen .44's for the Smith & Wesson Russian.

The night slipped by ever so slowly, yet Zed was no longer worried. A fight was coming and he was ready. He shifted his position with the cracking of dawn. Less than an hour more and the gentle clop of shod hooves and crackle of brush announced the posse's entrance on the opposite side of the open glade.

"Let 'em get in close for this scattergun," Zed whispered when he saw Blue anxiously lift his carbine. "You take the Ranger, I want Cooper. The hired man'll probably hightail it once they're put out of it, but get 'im if ya can."

Zed Rodel put the stock firmly against his shoulder and eared back both hammers as the enemy passed the halfway point. Grinning, Zed wished only that the two loads of shot in the twin barrels were of a larger size. Blast that pompous kid for not bringing that buckshot!

Suddenly his target halted. Cooper sat his saddle like a limp rag, but he spoke a word to the lawman next to him. The up-thrown head of the black gelding had given them away!

Rodel centered the bead on Tom's chest and tightened both triggers, wishing the distance was shorter but realizing the necessity of starting it now before the trio scattered like quail. From his peripheral vision he saw the Ranger start to bring his rifle from across his lap, and the outlaw leader hissed, "Now!"

Camp had been broken for the Ranger and his two deputies at the first hint of dawn, and Oates made a quick circle to look for any sign an intruder had been about the night before. He returned saying he'd found nothing but it paid to be careful in this work. They had better ride ready.

Tom stumbled when he took his first steps that

morning; it had taken a great effort to strap on the Colt earlier. His hands and feet didn't want to operate, and he was terribly dizzy. He hated having to let Jonas saddle and bridle his mustang.

Bretton handed Tom the reins and liked not how his friend seemed to be panting for breath at the slightest exertion. Upon seeing him fail at two attempts to mount, Jonas quickly boosted him into the leather. He heard Tom utter a curse then a thank you as he went to his own horse.

Oates was sitting the grulla and opened his mouth to recommend that Tom turn back with Bretton. The latter halted him with a shake of the head—it was too late for Cooper to seek medical aid now. Jonas fully expected his friend to fade before the next sunset. It was a sad thought, although realistic, and Jonas had always been the type to face the inevitable.

Cooper spurred his gelding ahead, swaying in the saddle. His right leg burned and throbbed, and he hadn't bothered to doctor it this morning. The appendage was covered in dark splotches from the hip down. He seemed to feel the poison all over his body.

He knew he was dying. There was an urgency in him because of it. If a confrontation would just begin, he could fight with recklessness. To the end.

Before a mile was covered he was slumping badly in the saddle. Unlike the other two, he did not ride with long gun drawn. He gripped the pommel with both hands, breaking out in a sweat at nausea and the strain to stay aboard the black.

The morning was bleak, gloomy. There was a damp mugginess in the air. A treefrog hollered for rain somewhere nearby.

Jonas Bretton pulled his sorrel up on Tom's near-side in case the man should fall, which appeared likely at every second. Jonas kept his eyes busy on the sur-roundings, and the trio continued along the dim track, timber and chaparral pressing in on either side so that they eventually had to proceed single file.

Cooper bounced and reeled in the lead.

From the dense forest they emerged and dropped down into a glade which was more open than the sa-vannahs normally seen in the South. Maybe an old house place, or field.

Bretton began to advise they go around its edge, but changed his mind and moved up by Tom again. There was no sign of horses having passed through the deep, dew-wet grass, and the fastest way on was straight ahead instead of skirting it. He tried to discern where the trail picked up on the far side, and couldn't.

Lord, don't let Bledsoe's directions fall short here!

Visions of Bell and little Stan flooded Cooper's near-delirious mind. Waves of grief and anger mud-dled his thoughts as well as torrents of pain. Past and present merged in confusion.

He snapped alert, however, when the mustang

halted of his own doing just beyond a pair of leaning sugar maples. The horse's head was up, ears pricked toward the tree line thirty yards on. Cooper glanced at his comrades on either side of him, and his hand moved sluggishly for his Colt.

His voice was thick, almost slurred. "Somethin' up yonder."

Then the stillness was ruptured by murderous gunfire.

Two shotgun blasts sounded almost as one and Tom and his horse went down in a thrashing mass from a hail of small lead pellets. About the same instant, Lonny Oates's skull was disintegrated into a gory pulp by a huge rifle ball placed right under his hat brim. The mouse-colored horse reared and lunged out from under the dead man . . . and Jonas Bretton was left unscathed but alone in the open on a shying mare.

Chapter Fifteen

Jonas reacted on impulse rather than ponderous judgment. With a shout that would have done a Rebel soldier proud, he put spurs to the sorrel and she bolted ahead like a good horse should.

Crouched low in the saddle, he charged forth, levering the '73 Winchester as fast as he could, both hands directing the gun, the knotted bridle reins draped over the pommel. His rapid bullets raked the timber line where gun smoke wafted up from the shots which had felled his two comrades, and he was rewarded with a cry of pain just before entering the woods.

Rodel and Blue were retreating in haste to the grove of hollies and their tethered mounts, the former man in the lead, left arm dangling. The Choctaw wheeled, knife in hand and cocked for a throw, upon hearing Bretton bearing down on him like a demon. Jonas was expecting such and, at the sidestep and pivot of the breed, he fired the rifle point-blank with one hand. The Indian spun and fell; Jonas raced by.

Zed Rodel was ten yards ahead. He'd gained his chestnut stallion and was yanking the reins free of a myrtle bush, brain intent on escaping the crazy black man who was fighting recklessly instead of hightailing like he'd presumed. The prancing stud horse further hindered Rodel's getting into the saddle with only one arm to pull up by. And the black man was coming!

Bretton sat the mare back on her haunches while using his right hand to jack a new load into the chamber. No sooner had the sorrel slid to a stop in a shower of forest litter and the Winchester's action clacked shut, than he was lining the sights on the struggling outlaw. Rodel had his left foot in the stirrup and was rising to the seat when the long gun cracked. He flung up his good arm and, having lost the grip on the pommel, thudded hard to the ground when the horse shied away. He lay still on his face.

Above the thrashing and braying of Blue's scared mule as it tore loose from its tether and raced off with the chestnut, Bretton heard a distinct, double click behind him. Quickly he reined around and felt the hot breath of a bullet on his cheek.

Five steps away the Choctaw sagged heavily on a

red oak, long black hair in disarray, shirtfront dark with blood, all the while trying to back the hammer of his Smith & Wesson again. Jonas carefully put another slug in the half-breed's blemished face and then guided the nervous mare forward to look down on the appalling corpse. Jonas's breathing was short and quick after the excitement.

"Go to the Spirit World and see what the Creator thinks of yo meanness, you sorry skunk!"

Bretton's swirling thoughts began to slow then. *Tom, I have to check Tom!* A quick look back to make sure Rodel still lay motionless, and he returned at a lope to the clearing full of carnage.

The glade reeked of destruction and the mare liked it no better than her master. One glance confirmed Oates was a lost cause, and Bretton didn't feel much better at Tom's prospects.

The man who'd been his friend and boss lay crumpled on his side, the infected leg pinned beneath the dead mustang. The copious amount of crimson and Tom's skin pallor was enough to prove demise long before Jonas climbed down to feel for a pulse. . . . Nothing.

He exhaled audibly and sat down hard by the deceased, tears spilling down his mahogany cheeks and his mount walking away from the smell of death.

* * *

Zed Rodel came to with his face pressed into the earth and his body racked with suffering. How long he'd been unconscious he couldn't be sure, yet it was still early in the day. The events of the morning entered his mind gradually in bits and pieces until everything was remembered.

After he listened for sounds that might tell of anyone nearby, he eased himself over on his back and almost screamed at the pain in spite of being careful. He rested for a time, sweating, breathing hard, and looking at the sun finally breaking through the clouds. His left arm had been broken above the elbow by the same wild projectile of the black man's which had knocked the 12 gauge from his grasp beyond where Blue lay dead yonder. But his hip, the torture in his hip was what was killing him.

He felt with his right hand and grimaced. Bretton's last shot had almost torn the scabbard from his gunbelt. It had struck the steel of the pistol within the holster, careened to the inside, and shattered his thigh bone just below the hip socket. Warm stickiness saturated the leg of his trousers. The pain was excruciating.

He began to take stock. His chestnut, even that confounded mule of Blue's, was gone. A hasty examination of his sidearm showed the cylinder was ruined by the slug now in his thigh; Rodel flung the useless weapon away in frustration, then grunted a curse at the pain the sudden movement caused him. Save a jay high up in the treetops, nothing stirred around him. No breeze, a stillness prevailed, and, the heat increased.

Therefore the remoteness of the place stood out in the outlaw's brain and was a horrible reminder of the trouble he was in. He had to get himself out of this mess!

He was panting with anger and fright, and he forced himself to calm when a pounding roar entered his head. Going into shock again would likely finish him. He was probably a dead man, anyway, but falling to pieces would only insure that. As with everything he'd done in his life, however it ended, he told himself this must be played out.

Sweat broke out over his entire body while plugging the hole in his thigh with the dirty bandanna from around his neck. The wound to his left arm had quit bleeding on its own, and he lay still, recovering a little from the agony throughout his person. He attempted to gain more composure with the deduction:

All right, Zed, let's get away from here just in case that nigger comes back. Find a place to cache, maybe get to the hideout.

Beyond that he refused to give consideration right now. Also he tried not to let himself dwell on the past. Guilt over his dastardly deeds nevertheless got through the wall of greed and self-importance he'd always been able to corral them in. A few years back, he had shot a young Cherokee through both knees and left him to die up on the Red River.

Teeth clenched against mental and physical anguish, Zed Rodel began to move. Using right arm and left leg, he went just inches at a time over the forest floor on his belly. Slowly, he fought distance, weakness, as well as searing pangs. Much was on his mind.

Not until Jonas Bretton had composed himself and pulled his dead friend from beneath the horse did he recall what Cooper had said the previous night. From his riddled vest Jonas retrieved an envelope, blood-stains and four tiny but deadly shot perforations on one end. In pencil on its side was written in small letters to conserve space:

Jonas,

For some time now, Bell and I have thought of you as family. Since I hired you on, you've done as much as the two of us to make the spread prosper, and you've earned more than just wages by the sweat of your brow. Bell and I both wanted to make you a partner in the Circle C. I intended to put your name on the papers as a wedding gift for you and Ruth.

If you are reading this, I am gone to be with the wife and son I love so much. In this you will find the deed and other documents signed over to you for full control of the homestead and stage station. Take them to the Maple Springs courthouse, and there should be no problem.

Even if this thing with Rodel is not over and done, go home and see to the outfit and the woman who waits for you. You've taken too many risks on my behalf already.

I cannot thank you enough for your friendship and loyalty.

Tom

Bretton started crying silently again upon reading the letter, and with shaking hands looked at the deed to the Circle-C property, verification of brand and earmarks on livestock, and contract with the stagecoach company. His scrawled name appeared blurry to him through the tears in his eyes, and he sobbed outright while gripping the shoulder of his dead friend. Gradually, he became resolute with what he had to do, and so went at it.

In that grassy branch bottom, in the shade of one of the twin maple trees, Jonas dug as decent a grave as possible with only a knife and tin plate for tools. There he lay Tom Cooper to rest wrapped in his blankets and with his weapons. A sadness every bit equal to that which Jonas had experienced when helping bury Bell and Stanly filled the black man's heart.

Before covering the corpse with the rich loam, he

whispered on a slight breeze, "Tom, you're the best friend I ever had, and I'm sho sorry fo' the hardships that was yours at the end."

While filling the grave Bretton thought of all the days he'd known the Coopers. They had gone to a dance proudly with him and Ruth more than once, and one time left with them when several people stated black folks weren't wanted at the "public" function. Yet before doing so Tom made it plain his views on the equality of every race.

Indeed, they had all been through good times and bad. One thing was clear to Jonas Bretton, however—the Coopers had been the greatest people to ride for. It had been an honor to know them.

And this gift he had been given . . . how many blacks in the South could hope for such a future?

The idea almost brought him to tears once more, but he choked it down and paused for a moment after he was done filling the grave. Tom hadn't really wanted to live without Bell and Stan. The man sure had seen a lot. And it was lamentable he hadn't gotten a better cut of the cards. What guarantee did any fellow have at an easy life, though?

At least the shotgun took him quicker than the blood poisoning would have. It ended his suffering.

Jonas would return here one day soon to erect an appropriate marker for Tom, and he'd do the same for the other two Coopers at the Circle C. He wished it would have been plausible to inter the family all in the same location at the homestead. Although Bretton's mama had taught him at an early age: "It ain't where this ol' sack of flesh and bones goes what counts, but the life in it." Sure Tom had faults, like everyone does, but there was no doubt in Jonas that he was with his folks in the World of their Maker now.

Hat back on his head, Bretton strode over to Lonny Oates. Staring down on the lifeless lawman, he felt sympathy for the sorrow the fellow's own associates and loved ones would feel. Lonny Oates had been a real man, a man with morals, but not impervious to the natural emotions of humans.

Daylight was burning, it was past noon now, and Jonas dreaded but realized what was his lot to do. The Ranger needed to be turned over to the nearest authorities, along with the outlaws. So he walked to retrieve his mare which had wandered to the edge of the glade, mounted her, and started off to collect all the other animals to pack the cadavers on.

The Ranger's horse he found just a couple of hundred yards to the other side of the shallow brook. Fording the waterway back to the battle site with the mouse-colored bronc in tow, Jonas entered the woods from which the desperados had begun their deadly ambuscade. He controlled both horses firmly as they passed the grisly form of the sprawled breed, and started on to pick up the trail of the chestnut and bay.

But wait, Jonas couldn't see Rodel.

His preoccupied mind returned to the possibility of danger, and he drew rein and scanned the surroundings. Maybe he wasn't looking in the right spot.

No, yonder was the myrtle bush the stallion had been tied to, and there was the criminal's hat. Yet no body in sight. And Jonas ought to have been able to see it from here!

A hasty looping of the grulla's reins on a laurel freed his right hand to shuck the Winchester from its scabbard as he nudged the sorrel ahead, cautiously. At the exact spot Zed Rodel had fallen from his frightened horse, Jonas halted and peered down at the earth.

He cursed at what he saw.

Chapter Sixteen

Dried blood and drag marks related a clear story to Bretton. Rodel hadn't been dead when he hit the ground, obviously hurt bad, but not dead. And now he had managed to crawl off like the wounded animal he was.

I should have placed my shot better! I ought to have made sure the snake was finished! The thoughts were turbulent but futile.

Bretton's gaze traced the sign forward, west, on toward the Neches. His eyes then narrowed as they slewed over the woods with meticulous care. He'd been occupied for quite a while since knocking Rodel from his steed. Was the bandit now lying somewhere expired from his wounds? If not, he could be lurking

176

as dangerous as a bloodied wildcat, cornered and frantic.

Sure, Jonas could see the discarded Colt where it lay damaged, and Rodel's shotgun was abandoned back near the open glade. Yet why couldn't the gang leader be in possession of a hideout weapon? A derringer like Bledsoe used, or perhaps one of those little pocket revolvers? Impossible to know, it was best to go with prudence.

Tom had directed Jonas in the letter to let this ride if it wasn't finished at his death, but not one second did Jonas give this consideration. Going by the blood Rodel had lost, and the difficult manner in which he was traveling, it was doubtful indeed that he would survive alone in this wilderness. Still . . . Bretton meant to be sure. He would not spend the rest of his days wondering if somehow, someway the killer of his *tayshas,* the Coopers, yet breathed.

Jonas checked to be certain a live round rested in the chamber of his Winchester. The sorrel shifted her weight under him, adjusted the bit in her mouth, and pawed the ground restively.

He nudged the mare ahead at an easy walk, thinking: *Just like tracking a varmint that's been preying on the livestock. I've done that plenty times before.*

The trail was anything but difficult to follow. Every few yards the quarry had had to pause and rest. His bleeding had almost stopped, yet his speed hadn't increased—he still clawed his way along.

Jonas Bretton rode alert and ready for action. The rifle's muzzle pointed at the treetops, its butt on its wielder's thigh. The man's dark eyes were never idle in one place; his ears took in and analyzed each sound, regardless of how minute. He went slow but steady. Nothing should go unnoticed, and he was fully aware of this while sitting the saddle rigidly, thumb resting on the rifle's hammer.

A mockingbird sang off to the left. A green lizard scurried up a tree and flashed the pink coloring under its neck at the man and horse's approach. Movement of an orange-and-black butterfly over a small patch of red clover drew Bretton's glance at the edge of his vision. The horse's hooves plodded softly on the carpet of shed leaves and pine needles.

The path led through what had clearly been a camp for the pair of owl hoots, although there were no remnants of a fire, then dropped abruptly toward the river bottom. Here the soil became increasingly dark and loamy, and the small stream widened a bit as it neared its junction with the Neches. The horse came to a halt, snorted, and shook its head upon entering a wide field of palmetto dotted with loblollies. Beyond, Jonas could make out the timbered edge of a lake or pond.

The fan-like grass grew about three feet high here and, save for narrow game trails through it, was very dense. First thing Jonas noticed was a spot of smeared crimson on a bunch of the green foliage near where some disturbed pine straw indicated Rodel's entrance to the tropical savannah. A short distance further, beneath one of the virgin pines, he made out a boot protruding from the grass.

Hoping the sharp leaves wouldn't cut the mare's legs too bad, Bretton neck-reined in a circle to come in sight of his quarry. Zed Rodel lay immobile on his side, eyes staring up at him through a glaze, and for an instant Jonas thought life had left him. Truly it was amazing the fellow had scratched and pulled himself these two hundred yards.

Then Rodel spoke hoarsely, "Finish it."

A bitter rage rushed to the surface of Bretton. He jerked the gun to his shoulder, sighted on the desperado's forehead just beneath his shock of dirty white hair, and prepared to drop the hammer on the .44-40 cartridge. . . . The level, almost-hopeful look on Zed's countenance made a revelation come over Jonas suddenly, however. With exaggerated calm he lowered the hammer and returned the weapon to the saddle boot.

"No," he stated, and his voice was hard, "yo life won't end so quick."

Over the pain-filled time it had taken Zed to get here, he had, for the first time ever, developed a real conscience. Every torturous inch he covered from where the black man shot him out of the saddle brought another evil he had committed to his mind. And he had begun to believe he was being punished by a God he'd never before believed in, fearing what might come before death—and after.

This was as far as he'd been able to travel toward his hideout before succumbing to weakness. The ox-bow lake and shanty were just a short distance on. Here in this expanse of palmetto, though, the physical anguish had become so great in the last hour that he didn't care any longer about a hereafter—if there even was one—only that he wanted out of *this* life. Many times during that hour he'd longed to have a firearm just so he could end his terrible suffering, himself, and when he had recognized Bretton through the haze in his brain, he voiced the desire for it to be done with.

But now the black fool was putting away the rifle which could end this so graciously fast, and he was reaching for something else.

Of a sudden the dull confusion left Zed's mind and was replaced by one thing, fear. A terrible fear of a thing he had always harbored a certain dread for—a noose!

The lasso Bretton lifted in a coil from his saddle horn quivered like a living thing as he shook out its loop. Rodel gave an unearthly shout, and, harnessing a reserve of energy from somewhere deep within, began to scramble in a vain attempt to escape. The terror he felt overcame all the pain in his body and he moved rather fast, unmindful to anything but the former, using his good arm and leg with much speed.

Jonas Bretton didn't rush himself. He made the throw just like he would have at a calf or big hog, forward and down. There was a faint hissing as the lariat sang through the air, then it encircled its target. Jonas made a quick dally on the horn, and the mare reacted instinctively, squatting, backing up without being told.

Rodel felt the stiff rope drop over his head and shoulders a split second before it bit in, pinning his arms and jerking him flat of his back. Breath left his lungs, yet he knew what was coming next and barely managed to grab hold of the rope in an attempt to prevent it from sliding up around his throat before Bretton wheeled his mount and spurred off. Ruined arm and leg flopping at unnatural angles, palmetto grass slicing his face with sharp edges, the outlaw was dragged along at break-neck speed.

A taut grin marred the black man's features as he pointed the horse back in the direction of the battlefield. The rage inside allowed him to relish every jolt and snag on the weighted end of the rope, and he strove for more speed while purposely riding through the thickest growths. Hat flew from his head, limbs and briars slapped horse and rider, but it was no more abuse than working stock dished out in these East

Texas woodlands, and Bretton did not halt until coming to a suitable sweet gum within ten feet of where Blue lay dead. Close by, the Ranger's grulla sidestepped on its tether as Rodel's limp form bounced to a stop in the dust and leaves raised by the sorrel.

Bretton hit the ground fast, hitched the mare's reins on a yaupon, and strode back to his prisoner. The notoriously feared bandit now made a pathetic sight—his bullet wounds were bleeding again profusely, and there was a multitude of cuts, scratches, and bruises to be seen on every exposed piece of his flesh. Although not one iota of remorse did Bretton feel for the battered man. In fact, he booted him roughly to see if he was dead.

"How's it feel to be on the bad end of the stick, Rodel?" he asked when the gang leader's eyes fluttered open.

For several seconds no sound came from the prisoner; Zed's vision and reasoning went in and out of focus. Pain, all was tremendous pain, and though oblivion tugged at him he found he could not sink into it. He groaned as strong hands cinched something around his neck. . . . It was then he became fully conscious with shocking perception of his dilemma.

"No! For . . . God's sake . . . just shoot me." It came out in croaks.

Bretton's dark face leered down at him; he was glad the outlaw wasn't dead yet. For a moment he'd worried the dragging might cheat him out of carrying out the rest of the sentence he had planned. If there had been an intense desire for vengeance back in Malloy upon looking at Bledsoe, the lust was doubled in Jonas now as he faced the devil who'd instigated it all.

Bretton's lips pulled back from large white teeth and out came the words: "Do you deserve such an easy way out, Rodel? By the Lord, I don't reckon.

"Two good men are dead yonder 'cause of you! And how many more? That one in the posse back in San Augustine, the two on the stage!

"Yeah, you remember 'em all, with Bell, little Stan, and the Hadzlot family on the way to meet yo Maker. But befo' ya face His wrath, you gonna face *mine!*"

With that, Jonas shook the opposite end of the rope free of the pommel and tossed it over a sturdy limb of the sweet gum. He acted in so quick a fashion that Zed could not grasp the noose with his good hand until Jonas had jerked him into a sitting position by a quick tug on the lariat.

"Yo gang's been sent to Hell ahead of ya, Rodel. They'll be waitin' on ya there!"

Zed struggled for air, got a finger in the hemp at his windpipe, and rasped, "Wait! T-take the money . . . but don't do this."

There was a part of Bretton which was really surprised. You wouldn't think such a hardened criminal would break. But all of Rodel's fearlessness and contempt for life melted when death was on him and he was helpless at the end of a string.

Bretton pondered this, the past days, and both Tom and Oates's kinds of justice. Were they all that different?

It all came down to this. And there was no sympathy in him. Why should there be?

Rodel was blubbering like a child now, from terror as much as pain. He repeated the plea to his captor.

Bretton met his miserable eyes firmly and demanded, "How many times have you ignored somebody beggin' you and yo buddies not to do somethin', you murderin' excuse for a man?" Then he put everything he had in his hard body into heaving on the rope.

Rodel was far beyond being able to stand, so his air was choked off even before his feet left the ground. Those cold eyes which had struck fear in so many a heart now held no speck of danger as they grew large at his own fright. His one finger in the noose helped him none, and he thrashed at the lack of air, face turning red then purple beneath disheveled white hair, and a roar growing in his skull. Indeed, in the time it took for Zed Rodel to die, the desperado thought of past, present, and future all in a frantic whirlwind of visions. A horde of violence punished by violence.

Leaning with a fiery passion against the weight on the other end of the lasso, Bretton watched until the man finished his last dance, the one which sent him into eternity and whatever awaited him there.

The corpse swung gently, a spur rowel turned to a stop, and the lariat squeaked on the tree branch. While tying off the hanging rope to the trunk, Bretton decided the buzzards and coyotes could darn well have Rodel and Blue. He didn't want a reward for the two cadavers, only to return the stolen money and the dead Texas Ranger to the proper officials. While striding calmly away from the repulsive smell and sight to fetch his hat, he concluded that all killers and marauders should be destroyed like the Zed Rodel gang.

It didn't bring the victims back, true enough. However, Rodel and his men would harm no one else.

It was late afternoon when Jonas was finally ready to head east. With some searching, he had rounded up the outlaws' mounts. The sacks of coin and currency he'd stripped from them with their gear, then started them off with a slap on the rump. He'd wrapped Oates in the man's ground sheet and packed him across his horse's saddle with the dirty money. Now, the loot-and corpse-laden grulla in tow, Jonas sat his blond mare taking a departing look at Cooper's grave.

A hollowness was in Jonas. For certain, killing was not to be looked upon as fun, but he had no regrets because he believed he had done the right thing. Yet the hunger for punishing revenge was gone in him—

it was over—replaced only by the deep loss which was his. Inner peace would take a while in coming.

In his mind's eye ran scenes of camaraderie with the Coopers back on the Circle C, amid leisure, toil, *and* strife. Always there had been and would still be a closeness. It would forever go unbroken.

He felt of the bundle of documents in his pocket, then murmured, "Ruth and I sho thank ya, Tom," and reined in the direction of the Sabine River and their home.